THIS DIARY BELONGS TO:

Nikki J. Maxwell

PRIVATE & CONFIDENTIAL

If found, please return to ME for REWARD!

(NO SNOOPING ALLOWED!!!☹)

ALSO BY
Rachel Renée Russell

Rachel Renée Russell

DORK diaries

Holiday Heartbreak

with Nikki Russell and Erin Russell

SIMON AND SCHUSTER

This edition published 2015

First published in Great Britain in 2013 by Simon and Schuster UK Ltd

First published in the USA in 2013 as *Dork Diaries 6: Tales from a Not-So-Happy Heartbreaker*,
by Aladdin, an imprint of Simon & Schuster Children's Publishing Division.

3 5 7 9 10 8 6 4 2

Simon & Schuster UK Ltd
1st Floor, 222 Gray's Inn Road
London WC1X 8HB

Simon & Schuster Australia, Sydney
Simon & Schuster India, New Delhi

A CIP catalogue record for this book
is available from the British Library.

PB ISBN: 978-1-4711-9810-6
eBook ISBN: 978-0-85707-939-8

Printed and bound by CPI Group (UK) Ltd, Croydon, CR0 4YY

MIX
Paper from
responsible sources
FSC® C020471

www.simonandschuster.co.uk
ww.simonandschuster.com.au

www.dorkdiaries.co.uk

To my aunt Betty and uncle Phil.
Thank you for always being there for me
and for treating me like your pretend daughter.
I love you both dearly!

ACKNOWLEDGMENTS

Wow! It's hard to believe we now have a Dork Diaries Book 6! I would like to thank the following members of Team Dork:

My DORKALICIOUS fans all over the world! Each and every one of you is very special to me!

Daniel Lazar, my dream agent (thank you for supporting my sometimes wacky ideas); Liesa Abrams Mignogna (a.k.a. Batgirl!), my fabulous and fun editor (who almost makes this NOT seem like work); Jeanine Henderson, my super-fast-and-talented art director (who survived this book); Torie, my very organised pen pal; and Deena Warner, my website magician.

Mara Anastas, Carolyn Swerdloff, Matt Pantoliano, Katherine Devendorf, Paul Crichton, Fiona Simpson, Lydia Finn, Alyson Heller, Lauren Forte, Karin Paprocki, Lucille Rettino, Mary Marotta and the entire sales team, and everyone else at Aladdin/Simon & Schuster. I'm so lucky YOU chose ME!

Maja Nikolic, Cecilia de la Campa, and Angharad Kowal, my foreign rights agents at Writers House for steadily recruiting new Dorks, one country at a time.

And last but not least, my entire ADORKABLE family! Thank you for being the inspiration for this series.

Always remember to let your inner DORK shine through!

SATURDAY, FEBRUARY 1

OMG! I'm suffering from the worst case of CRUSH-ITIS ever!

This morning I had these fluttery butterflies in my stomach that were making me feel SUPERnauseous ☹! But in a really GOOD way ☺!

I felt SO insanely happy I could just . . . VOMIT sunshine, rainbows, confetti, glitter and . . . um . . . those yummy little Skittles thingies!

I still can't believe my crush, Brandon, actually texted me last night after I left his birthday party.

And you'll NEVER guess what happened??!!

HE ASKED ME OUT TO CRAZY BURGER!! SQUEEE ☺!!

And yes, I know it's NOT like a real date or anything. But STILL!

I was SO elated, I blasted my FAVE music and danced around my bedroom like a MANIAC. . .

Hey! I was beyond FIERCE! I was an air-guitar-playing, dancing machine!

After dancing in my room for an entire hour, I was so tired I could barely breathe.

That's when I collapsed into a wheezing, sweat-soaked mass of body odour and sheer exhaustion.

GASP!!
COUGH!!
HACK!!

A very *HAPPY* wheezing, sweat-soaked mass of body odour and sheer exhaustion.

ME, WITH A BIG FAT DORKY
SMILE PLASTERED ACROSS MY FACE!!

WHY? Because any minute now, Brandon was going to contact me so we could make plans to hang out at Crazy Burger.

SQUEEEEEE ☺!

So I snuggled into a comfy chair, stared at my phone and waited patiently for his call.

I WAITED . . .

And WAITED . . .

(2 hours later)

And WAITED . . .

(4 hours later)

And WAITED!!

(6 hours later)

Before I knew it, it was bedtime. I felt like I'd been waiting FOREVER. . . !!

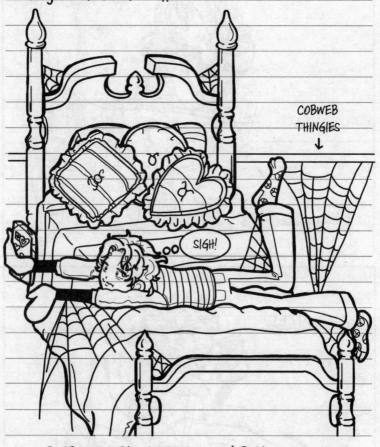

ME, FLOPPED ACROSS MY BED, SULKING

But no call! No email! Not even a text message! I even checked my phone to make sure the battery thingy hadn't run down or something.

Unfortunately, my last call was from my BFFs, Chloe and Zoey. They had called me late last night with some REALLY juicy gossip.

Apparently, someone had showed up at Brandon's party unexpectedly to drop off a present for him shortly after I had left.

You'll NEVER guess who it was!

MACKENZIE !!

Okay, I'll admit it was really nice and sweet of her to do that. But she had totally overlooked one very important little detail . . .

SHE WASN'T INVITED!
!!

Which meant MISS THANG had basically CRASHED Brandon's party! Like, WHO does that?!

My BFFs told me that MacKenzie was twirling her

hair, giggling and flirting with Brandon like crazy.
Then she got superserious and asked to talk to him
PRIVATELY about something really important!

JUST GREAT ☹! Now I'm really starting to ~~worry~~
PANIC!

What if MacKenzie told him some awful lies about
me so he wouldn't want to be friends anymore?!!

She's always talking about me behind my back and
saying stuff like, "Nikki's a hopelessly insecure,
fashion-challenged, diary-obsessed DORK!"

Which is so NOT true! Well . . . maybe it's a little
true. Okay! Actually, a LOT true. But STILL!!

WHY did all of this have to happen just when
Brandon and I were about to have our very first
date-that-really-isn't-a-date ☹?!

PLEASE, PLEASE, PLEASE,
PLEASE, PLEASE let Brandon call me
tomorrow!!

SUNDAY, FEBRUARY 2

I've been awake now for

7 hours, 11 minutes, and 39 seconds

and Brandon STILL hasn't called ☹!!

I'm starting to worry that something really BAD happened to him.

I think he sincerely WANTED to call me.

And he sincerely TRIED to call me.

But he just COULDN'T!

Because maybe . . . he got, um . . . abducted . . . by . . .

ALIENS ☹!!

Hey, don't laugh!!

It could have actually happened. . . !!

"I CAN'T BELIEVE THIS IS HAPPENING! I DROPPED
MY PHONE AND NOW I CAN'T CALL NIKKI!"

In spite of the fact that I was still suffering from a severe case of crush-itis AND having a really BAD day, my parents MADE me babysit my little sister, Brianna.

Just so they could go to a movie together! Like, how INSENSITIVE is that?! Sometimes I think Mom and Dad need to take a parenting class or something.

The last time I tried to talk to Brandon on the phone with Brianna around, it was a total disaster. She actually told him about my hairy legs and crusty eye boogers. It was SO humiliating!

Lately, Brianna has been totally obsessed with those diva hair salon shows on TV. And get this! She actually calls herself Miss Bri-Bri, Fashionista Hairstylist to the Stars!

I was shocked to see her sneaking into my parents' bathroom and stealing shampoo and perfume and stuff. It was like I had personally witnessed a MIRACLE!

Brianna was FINALLY trying to improve her very NASTY hygiene ☺!

WOO-HOO!

But later, when I peeked inside Brianna's room, I discovered she was MISSING!

And in her place was this strange little woman.

She was wearing fake diamond cat-eye glasses, a long scarf, four-sizes-too-big satin slippers and a kiddie painting apron filled with Mom's designer makeup collection.

I didn't know WHO the heck she was.

I wanted to scream, "Who are YOU? And what have you done with MY little sister?!"

But my gut told me to run away FAST and call the POLICE!

Then she smiled at me really big and said . . .

"BONJOUR, MISS NIKKI!
WELCOME TO SALON BRIANNA!!"

I was halfway down the hall before Brianna caught up with me. She grabbed my arm and dragged me back toward her room.

"Dah-ling! Where are you going?! Don't be skurd!" Brianna said in an awful fake French accent that sounded more like a six-year-old Arnold Schwarzenegger.

"You're playing with Mom's new makeup and perfume?! You DO realize she's going to KILL you when she gets home! Right?!" I scolded her.

"Never mind zat, dah-ling! You are Miss Bri-Bri's next appointment! Wee! Wee! Come! Come!" she said, pushing me into her ~~desk~~ salon chair.

Kidz Bop music was playing in the background. And she'd drawn the most hideous hairstyle posters and hung them on her wall to help set the mood of a trendy, upscale salon.

Those posters should've been a WARNING to me about Miss Bri-Bri's hairstyling abilities. I couldn't resist coming up with catchy names for each one. . .

"Don't worry, dah-ling," Miss Bri-Bri said. "I'm going to make you BOOTY-FUL! For your little friend Brandon. Yes?!"

For BRANDON?!!! I blushed profusely.

Hey! It was JUST a pretend makeover with Miss Bri-Bri, Fashionista Hairstylist to the Stars!

What could possibly go WRONG?

"Okay. As long as it's ONLY pretend!" I grumped.

If I was lucky, this would keep Brianna occupied until Mom and Dad got home. And it was way LESS dangerous than us baking cookies and almost burning down the house. AGAIN!

"YAAAY!!! My first customer!" ~~Brianna~~ Miss Bri-Bri cheered. "Before I start, dah-ling, would you like something to drink? Juicy Juice? Hawaiian Punch? Chocolate milk?"

"Chocolate milk would be nice," I answered.

"Hans! Go get our customer, Miss Nikki, a glass of le chocolate milk! Extra cold!" she commanded, looking at the teddy bear in the chair next to mine.

The bear . . . I mean . . . Hans . . . didn't move.

"Well?!" She glared at him. "Don't just sit there! Go get zee milk for her. Now! PLEASE!!"

Then she turned to me and laughed uncomfortably. "Please excuse my assistant. Hans is new here. He speaks la French, but very little English."

I looked at the teddy bear, looked back at her, and raised an eyebrow. "Um . . . okay?" I replied.

"I know just what to do with your hair, dah-ling!" Brianna said as she draped a ~~bath towel~~ smock around my shoulders. "Now, just relax and let Miss Bri-Bri work her magic! Yes? Hans, would you please grab that magazine and give it to— Oh, never mind! I'll do it myself!"

Brianna handed me a trendy teen fashion magazine to read, just like in a real salon. I was impressed. Until I realized she had swiped MY new *Teen Thing* mag from my room. The little THIEF!!

But I had to admit, Miss Bri-Bri, Fashionista Hairstylist to the Stars, seemed to know her stuff. . .

ME, READING WHILE MISS BRI-BRI DOES MY HAIR

That's when I came across this very intriguing
article about — you guessed it — GUYS!!

HOW TO KNOW IF A GUY IS JUST *NOT* INTO YOU!

1. He agrees to a date and then rudely cancels at the very last minute.

2. He simply texts you an apology instead of telling you in person.

3. Suddenly he's always too busy to spend any time with you.

4. When you try to talk about your relationship, he just walks away.

5. He's spending way too much time with another girl.

That magazine article was just . . . SHOCKING!

Only a guy who was a total LOSER would do those things.

I felt really lucky I didn't have to deal with "DDD" (Dysfunctional Dude Drama) in my OWN life.

I ripped out the magazine page, folded it, and stuck it in my pocket. You know, for future reference. Just in case.

Suddenly I felt a tug on my hair.

Then a huge yank!

"Ouch!" I yelped. "Brianna, WHAT are you doing?!"

"Making you booty-ful, dah-ling! Zere eez no problem at all! No, no! Don't worry, please!"

In spite of her assurances, I sensed a little uncertainty in that jacked-up accent of hers.

Next I felt another slight tug and then . . . SNIP!

A chopped-off braid landed in my lap!

I gasped!

Then, with a trembling hand, I picked up the braid and PRAYED that it belonged to someone else.

Like maybe Hans, that lazy, French-speaking teddy bear assistant!

"What is THIS?!" I yelled at Brianna as I stared at it in horror.

"Nut-ting! Nut-ting at all. I throw away! Yes?" She snatched the braid from me and tossed it over her shoulder. "There! All gone!"

"Brianna! Give me that mirror! Now! Or this game is SO over!" I screeched, my eyeballs bulging.

Brianna handed it to me and giggled nervously.

BRIANNA HANDS ME THE MIRROR

Well, I took one look in that mirror and . . .

OMG ☹!!

I don't have the words to describe how BAD my hair looked.

Maybe, um . . .

HIDEOUS-A-LICIOUS!

Which is, like, ten times worse than just plain ol' HIDEOUS!

I couldn't believe the HOT MESS I saw in that mirror.

I thought my eyes were going to rupture and bleed from being exposed to such awesomely wretched . . .

UGLINESS!!

AAAAAAH!!

(THAT WAS ME SCREAMING!)

And the back was even worse! Just as I had
suspected, a large chunk of hair was missing. . .

→
MISSING
HAIR CHUNK

I seriously considered crawling around on the floor
until I found my severed braid.

Then I'd place it in a bucket of ice and rush to
the nearest emergency room to see if doctors could
somehow surgically reattach it. . .

27

"DOCTORS, PLEASE! YOU NEED TO DO
EMERGENCY SURGERY TO REATTACH
MY BRAID BEFORE MY, UM . . .
HAIR-FOLLICLE THINGIES . . . DIE!"

"My hair! My poor hair!" I sobbed. "Brianna, I'm so mad at you right now I could just . . . ARRRRRGGH!!"

"Dah-ling! Please! Calm down! This is a no-tears salon! But tipping IS allowed!" Miss Bri-Bri grinned as she held out her hand. "Got any loose change?"

She expected payment?!!

I was beyond DISGUSTED!

Sorry! But I'd had quite enough of Brianna and her:

1. phoney-baloney French accent.

2. ugly haircuts.

3. lazy, no-good assistant, Hans!

"Hair styled by Miss Bri-Bri is always booty-ful! I take a PICTURE of your booty!" Brianna said as she grabbed my phone off of her dresser and set it to camera mode. . .

A blinding flash went off and I couldn't see a thing.

Which was lucky for Brianna! Because right then I was so mad I wanted to give HER a supercute and stylish haircut. With a chain saw!

"Nikki, is this the button you press to send stuff?" Brianna asked. "I wanna send this picture to Chloe and Zoey so I can get more customers!"

That's when I went from furious to LIVID! "Brianna, are you NUTS?! You'd better NOT send that picture of me to ANYONE!"

"Why not? I need more customers to get more money. How am I supposed to pay Miss Penelope to be my shampoo girl?!"

"Just give me back my phone!!" I screamed, and snatched it from her.

"Mommy says sharing is a good thing!" Brianna shouted and grabbed it back.

We yelled at each other and tussled over the phone for what seemed like FOREVER...

31

ME AND BRIANNA,
FIGHTING OVER MY PHONE

That is, until we heard the phone go *CLICK!* and then *BEEP!* I had a total meltdown right there on the spot!!

There's a saying that a picture's worth a thousand words.

Well, mine is worth a million laughs!

I looked like a PSYCHOTIC, HOMELESS, um . . . CLOWN who'd . . . accidentally stuck her finger in an ELECTRICAL SOCKET!

Chloe and Zoey immediately sent me "LOL" texts in response.

They were always texting me funny pictures.

But I was SUPERworried that after Brandon saw that photo, he'd be so freaked out, he'd NEVER want to hang out with me again!

He still hadn't called, emailed, or even texted me all weekend.

I was seriously contemplating whether or not to try and superglue that hair chunk back on or just part my hair differently to try to hide the bald spot when my phone chimed.

OMG!

I almost jumped out of my skin. It was a text from BRANDON!

Finally!!

SQUEEE ☺!!!

My heart was pounding as I read his text message.

I actually read it, like, three times before his very cryptic message finally sank in.

OH.

NO.

HE.

DIDN'T!!

I closed my eyes tightly and . . . groaned in despair . . . like a mortally wounded, um . . . gorilla or something. How could he do this to me?!!

I immediately recognised Brandon's behaviour from that magazine article "How to Know if a Guy Is Just *NOT* Into You!":

1. He agrees to a date and then rudely cancels at the very last minute.

2. He simply texts you an apology instead of telling you in person.

I crossed off both #1 and #2 from the list.

Maybe Brandon was too embarrassed to be seen with a slightly goofy, majorly insecure girl who WASN'T a CCP (Cute, Cool & Popular) like MacKenzie.

Or maybe the thought of my dad's exterminator van with a plastic bug on it the size of a large hog had made him lose his appetite.

Permanently!

Suddenly I felt so . . . STUPID!!

What made me think Brandon would WANT to go anywhere with ME?!!

Anyway, for the past hour I've been working on a new Crush Rejection Equation to try and figure out what happened.

The calculations are SUPERcomplex. And who knows! All of my hard work on this equation might one day earn me the Nobel Prize in maths. . .

MY PHONE →

BRANDON PLUS NIKKI DIVIDED BY A RANDOM TEXT MESSAGE EQUALS . . . HEARTBREAK!

Why is all of this guy stuff SO confusing?!

I guess I could write in to my Miss Know-It-All advice column and ask myself for romantic advice.

Especially since my two friends Chloe and Marcie begged me to let them take over my column for the entire month of February.

They're doing a special Miss Know-It-All Crush Crisis Love Advice column, which means I have the entire month off.

Anyway, here's my letter. . .

Dear Miss Know-It-All,

Why is love such a CRUDDY thing?

Help!

A Brokenhearted Dork ☹!

MONDAY, FEBRUARY 3

I'm still pretty bummed out over Brandon's text message.

I really wanted to give him the benefit of the doubt, but the magazine article wouldn't let me.

I planned to just pretend the whole Crazy Burger thing had never happened and TOTALLY ignore him.

However, when I arrived at school, the first thing I noticed was that ALL of the guys were acting really strange. Even the normally rowdy jocks were huddled together in small groups, quietly talking among themselves.

But mostly, everyone was staring nervously at some huge commotion down the hall.

WHAT was going on??! And WHERE were all the GIRLS?!

Okay, this was just too . . . WEIRD.

While all of the guys stood there gawking, I decided to go down the hall and investigate. . .

OMG! I could NOT believe my eyes!!

Practically every girl in the entire school was part of this huge crowd in line for tickets to the Sweetheart Dance.

Jordyn, the girl who sits behind me in geometry, showed me her tickets and excitedly filled me in. . .

"NIKKI, THIS IS THE MOST POPULAR DANCE OF THE YEAR! BUT MAKE SURE YOU GET YOUR TICKETS SOON BECAUSE THEY USUALLY SELL OUT IN A FEW DAYS!"

She was right about the dance being really popular. The line was so long that it flowed past the office, wrapped around the corner near the library and extended beyond the cafeteria door. It looked like the entrance to a sold-out Justin Bieber concert! But get this. . . !!

It was GIRLS ASK THE GUYS!

Of course, I totally FREAKED! Unfortunately, the ONLY guy I am even remotely interested in couldn't even stand to eat a burger with me ☹!

I was so NOT asking him to some Sweetheart Dance!!

All of this gushy sweetheart stuff was getting on my last nerve. So I decided to go to my locker and vent in my diary before my first class.

But THAT was a really BAD idea!

MacKenzie had bedazzled her locker with so many sparkly red and pink hearts, it practically blinded me. Even her lip gloss was red and glittery!

← ME

HOW in the world was I supposed to write in my
diary when all of HER very tacky BLING-BLING
was, um . . . BLING-BLINGING all over the place?!!

I couldn't believe what happened next. That girl wrinkled her nose and then sprayed her Pretty Poison designer perfume all over me, accidentally-on-purpose.

Like, WHO does that?! Finally, I just totally lost it.

"PLEASE, MacKenzie! Could you be more careful where you're spraying that stuff?"

"Sorry, Nikki! It's just that your odour is especially pungent today. And I don't have a can of disinfectant spray."

"Personally, I'd prefer disinfectant. What's the name of that perfume you're wearing? Flea-'n'-Tick Repellent?" I shot back.

Calling MacKenzie a mean girl is an understatement. She's a shark in lip gloss, skinny jeans and platform heels.

Suddenly she turned around and got all up in my face like spot cream or something. . .

"SO, NIKKI, ARE YOU GOING TO THE
SWEETHEART DANCE? OH, MY BAD!
THEY DON'T ADMIT ANIMALS!"

"Actually, MacKenzie, that stank you're smelling is
not me. It's coming from your mouth. You're obviously
suffering from a severe case of BLABBER-ITIS! Is
that stuff contagious?"

MacKenzie glared at me with her beady little eyes.
"Admit it, Nikki! You're just jealous because Brandon

liked the digital camera I gave him for his birthday A LOT better than YOUR stupid gift certificates to CRUDDY BURGER."

"It's not CRUDDY Burger. It's CRAZY Burger!" I said, wondering how she even knew about it. Had Brandon told her we were going to Crazy Burger together to use his gift certificates?

"Whatever! Your gift was SO tacky! I got the camera so Brandon can take pictures of me when I'm crowned Sweetheart Princess. And I've already asked him to the dance, so don't even think about it."

I just blinked my eyes in shock! MacKenzie had already asked Brandon to the dance???!!!!

Did he say YES or NO?!! Or MAYBE? She had very conveniently left out THAT little detail.

However, I had to admit, everything was starting to make perfect sense.

When MacKenzie had asked to talk to Brandon in

private at his birthday party, it was probably to invite him to the Sweetheart Dance!

And if they were going to the dance together, there was NO WAY she'd want him hanging out with ME at Crazy Burger.

So he had sent me that text ☹!

I closed my eyes, sighed deeply and bit my lip.

Then an unexpected wave of anger rushed over me.

MacKenzie is NOT the boss of me! It's a free country! I can ask WHOEVER I want to the dance.

And yes, Brandon had just stood me up.

But STILL!

There was NO reason why I couldn't just totally HUMILIATE myself by ASKING him anyway. Right?!

WRONG!! If MacKenzie and Brandon want to be together, I'm NOT going to stand in their wa—

That's when MacKenzie rudely interrupted the deep conversation I was having with myself. "BTW, Nikki, just a friendly little reminder! Make sure you vote for ME for Sweetheart Princess on February fourteenth! Everybody else is going to. I'm SOOO popular!" MacKenzie gushed.

Then she flipped her hair and sashayed away. I just HATE it when that girl sashays!

I was really upset that MacKenzie was trying to undermine my friendship with Brandon. AGAIN!

What if I asked him to the dance too?! Then he'd be forced to choose!

TWO desperate girls and ONE guy! Just GREAT ☹!

Of course, this left me with one very obvious and compelling question.

WHY in the world would MacKenzie ask ME to vote for HER for Sweetheart Princess when it's so obvious that she HATES my guts?!

All of this is mind-boggling!! And my mind is so BOGGLED, I seriously need to talk to my BFFs, Chloe and Zoey.

They were the ONLY other girls in the entire school whose brains did NOT turn into MUSH today from Sweetheart FEVER!!

I'm already SICK of Valentine's Day, and it's still two weeks away!

!

TUESDAY, FEBRUARY 4

Okay, I was TOTALLY wrong about Chloe and Zoey NOT having Sweetheart Fever.

They're both so obsessed with the dance that their brains are way MUSHIER than all of the other lovesick, mushy-brained girls at school ☹!

Of course, this was a shocking discovery.

I first noticed it in gym class during our swimming section at the WCD High School pool.

We were supposed to be in the water warming up and doing laps for conditioning.

But Chloe and Zoey were SO excited about the upcoming dance that we spent the ENTIRE hour just hanging out on the side of the pool, gossiping about it.

Which was fine by me since I'm not that good at swimming anyway. . .

CHLOE, ZOEY AND ME, IN GYM CLASS
SWIMMING LAPS IN THE POOL
(WELL, SORT OF)

Even though they both wanted to go to the dance REALLY, REALLY badly, they had NOT got tickets yet.

And guess WHY?! THEY didn't want to go UNLESS I went TOO!

I was like, "Come on, GUYS! If you both want to go, you should just do it! I'm sure it'll be really fun and exciting!"

"But it wouldn't be the same without you, Nikki!" Chloe said sullenly.

"Come on, Nikki! We're BFFs. We're supposed to do EVERYTHING together!" Zoey whined.

That's when I totally lost my patience with those two and yelled at them. "Really?! So if I jumped off a cliff, then you two would do it also? And what if I accidentally got hit by a bus — would you want to get hit by a bus too? Come on, girlfriends! We're BFFs! Not CLONES! I think it's time for you to grow up and get a LIFE!"

But of course I said all of that inside my head so no one else heard it but me.

Even though they can sometimes be a little annoying, I would NEVER hurt their feelings on purpose. After all, they ARE my BFFs!

"Besides, I'm SURE you're DYING to ask your boo, Brandon, to the dance!" Chloe said, and started making kissy sounds.

"Yeah!" Zoey giggled. "Everyone saw you two making GOO-GOO eyes at each other at his birthday party."

Did I mention the fact that sometimes my BFFs can be a little SUPERannoying?

"We were NOT making goo-goo eyes at each other!" I whisper-shouted as I flushed with embarrassment.

"Were TOO!" Chloe and Zoey teased.

"Were NOT!"

"Were TOO!"

"Were NOT!"

"Were TOO!"

It seemed as if our silly little argument went on, like, FOREVER!

"Okay, already!" I said, finally giving in. "So maybe Brandon and I goo-goo-eyed each other once or twice. But it wasn't on purpose. Mostly." Then I quickly changed the subject. "But what I'M dying to know is who you'd like to ask to the dance. Come on, girlfriends! Spill it!"

Chloe and Zoey blushed profusely.

"Actually, I did have someone in mind. But since we aren't going, I guess that means you'll NEVER know!" Chloe said smugly, and gave me the stink eye.

"Same here!" Zoey said, and playfully stuck her tongue out at me. "For ME to know and YOU to find out!"

CHLOE AND ZOEY VERY RUDELY REFUSE
TO TELL ME WHO THEY'RE CRUSHING ON.

Did I mention the fact that sometimes my BFFs
are a MAJOR PAIN? But it was a NO-BRAINER!
They've been crushing on Jason and Ryan, two CCP
guys, for, like, FOREVER. DUH!!

Anyway, even though Chloe and Zoey were really
looking forward to the dance, the three of us
decided not to go.

I was actually kind of relieved, since I didn't have a date.

I decided not to tell them about the whole Crazy Burger fiasco and Brandon's text message. Or that he and MacKenzie were probably going to the Sweetheart Dance together.

To be honest, I wasn't all that sure about my friendship with Brandon anymore.

So I TOTALLY FREAKED when he came up to my locker today acting all nice and friendly. Kind of like nothing had ever happened between us.

He was like, "Hey, Nikki! Oh, by the way, about Crazy Burger. I just wanted to tell you—"

And I was like, "Really, Brandon. No problem at all. Just FORGET about it!"

Then he looked a little surprised and was like, "Wait, I really need to explain. I wanted to hang out with you last weekend. But things got a little crazy. After MacKenzie dropped by my birthday party, I realised that I—"

And I was like, "I know! You were superbusy. But I really don't have time to talk right now. I've got a lot of STUFF to do! SORRY! Sound familiar?!" Then I folded my arms and just glared at him with this aggravated look on my face like, *WHAT?!!*

And he stuck his hands in his pockets and just stared at ME with this perplexed look on his face like, *HUH?!!!*

It seemed like all of that glaring and staring went on, like, FOREVER.

Finally, Brandon shrugged. "Um, okay. I guess I better get to class. Later, Nikki."

Then he just walked away! Like, WHO does that?!

How could he leave right in the middle of a serious discussion about our friendship? It was like he didn't even care.

That's when the magazine article "How to Know if a Guy Is Just *NOT* Into You!" popped into my head again.

I took it out of my backpack and read it over. Then I crossed off another item on the list. . .

4. When you try to talk about your relationship, he just walks away.

Things had gone from BAD to WORSE!

But OMG! What Brandon did later that night was totally unexpected.

He sent me not one, but TWO more text messages!!

Did I get a sincere, heartfelt apology about that whole Crazy Burger fiasco?

NO! WAY!

* * * * *
FROM BRANDON:
&&&&&&kkkkkkkwwwbbbbbbbb@@@
8:12 p.m.
* * * * *
FROM BRANDON:
Sorry, Nikki! I just butt-dialled you. Please ignore.
8:14 p.m.
* * * * *

AARRGH ☹!!

Back in November I put together a band called Actually, I'm Not Really Sure Yet (formerly known as Dorkalicious), and we performed in the Westchester Country Day Middle School talent show.

One of the grand prizes was a chance to participate in a reality TV show/talent boot camp called . . .

It's produced by the famous TV producer Trevor Chase, who was also a celebrity judge for our WCD talent show.

I was disappointed when MacKenzie's dance group, Mac's Maniacs, won and we didn't.

Hey, I just thought my band was FANTASTIC!

And apparently, so did Mr Chase. He said his boot camp was for amateurs and beginners. But he felt our band was already fairly polished and wouldn't benefit from it.

Of course that was a BIG compliment! But it gets even better.

He said he was interested in recording an original song that we'd written and performed, called "Dorks Rule!"

We're supposed to meet with him on Saturday, February 8. How COOL is THAT?!

So today after school we had practice at Theo's house.

It was always fun hanging out with Chloe, Zoey, Violet, Theo and Marcus. Although, things between Brandon and me were just plain . . . AWKWARD ☹!

He kept staring at me the whole time with this strange look on his face. Like I was a puzzle he was trying to figure out or something.

But the weird thing was that it seemed like everyone else had an extreme case of the giggles. I started to wonder what was in that hot chocolate we were drinking.

I was trying to conduct a serious meeting about the future of our band, and they just kept laughing and cracking jokes.

Well, everyone except Brandon. He just continued to stare at me, which made me SUPERnervous.

"COME ON, GUYS! STOP GOOFING AROUND!"

Anyway, our practice went really well. We totally ROCKED our song "Dorks Rule!"

MY BAND, PERFORMING "DORKS RULE!"

After practice, I noticed Chloe and Marcus, and Zoey and Theo, were actually FLIRTING with each other!!

That's when it occurred to me that they BOTH made really CUTE couples! The best part was that Marcus and Theo seemed to REALLY like Chloe and Zoey.

Unlike those two slimy CCP guys Jason and Ryan. It was quite obvious that they only hung around my BFFs to do MacKenzie's EVIL bidding. They had successfully manipulated Chloe and Zoey in the past.

But I am NOT about to let it happen AGAIN!

I don't know what that witch MacKenzie is cooking up in her cauldron. But she'd better hold on to her pointy little hat if she comes rolling up on me again! WHY? Because I'm so SICK of her and her two evil little flying monkeys, Jason and Ryan.

MACKENZIE AND HER EVIL FLYING
MONKEYS, JASON AND RYAN

That's when the most FABULOUS idea popped into my head.

Chloe and Zoey would absolutely DIE if I surprised them with tickets to the Sweetheart Dance!

And they TOTALLY deserve it too. They are FOREVER rescuing MY butt from one disaster or another.

Even though I'm not going to the dance, there's no reason why THEY can't go!

And Theo and Marcus would be the perfect dates for them!

SQUEEE ☺!!

Am I not BRILLIANT??!!!

After I got home, I texted them both and told them I had a GINORMOUS surprise for them. Of course they begged me to tell them what it is.

But I told them I'm going to give it to them tomorrow during fifth period since we all work together in the library as shelving assistants.

Chloe and Zoey are SUPERlucky to have ME as a BFF!

I STILL can't get Brandon's sad, slightly puzzled puppy-dog face out of my head.

Since he's been acting genuinely sorry about the whole Crazy Burger thing, just MAYBE I'll consider buying tickets for US, too!

☺!!

P.S. Assuming, of course, he's NOT already going with MacKenzie!

I was so excited about my BIG surprise for Chloe and Zoey that I could barely eat breakfast.

Thank goodness I had just enough money for six tickets saved up from babysitting Brianna and my allowance.

I begged my mom to drop me off at school ten minutes earlier than usual so I could buy the Sweetheart Dance tickets before Chloe and Zoey arrived.

As I rushed down the hall, I passed a bunch of girls who had obviously just purchased their tickets.

Several girls kissed their tickets, while others just stared and giggled hysterically. One girl twirled in circles and another jumped for joy.

OMG! It was like being in the hallway of a mental institution or something!

But the good news was, it looked like tickets were STILL available! Woo-hoo!

However, this is what happened when I tried to buy mine . . .

I couldn't believe my ROTTEN luck!

"No more tickets are available?! Are you SURE?!"
I asked desperately.

"Since we're having a special catered dinner for the
dance, we had to turn in a figure for the number
of students attending one week before the event.
Unfortunately, our adviser placed the telephone call
with the final headcount five minutes ago. So we
can't sell any more tickets. Sorry!" said Brittany,
the cheerleading captain, as she pulled their poster
off the wall.

"Just GREAT!" I muttered.

Then I turned around and rushed straight down the
hall to the nearest girls' bathroom.

I locked myself in a stall and waited until the
bathroom was completely empty. Then, in a very
CALM and MATURE manner, I did what any normal
girl would do in my exact same situation. . .

I had a really good SCREAM 😣...!

Which, for some strange reason, always makes me feel a lot better ☺!

But now I had a whole NEW problem.

Chloe and Zoey were expecting this HUGE surprise.

And NOW I didn't have anything to give them!!

Which meant they were going to be SUPER-disappointed.

How CRUDDY would THAT be??!!

I dug through my locker, trying to find something to give them.

A mouldy peanut butter sandwich?

My favourite not-from-the-mall old hoodie?

An opened pack of tissues?

A half-used tube of lip gloss?

My situation was hopeless!

Maybe I could give them something really unusual.

For me, anyway.

Something that would require honesty, integrity and maturity.

Like maybe . . . the TRUTH?!

"I'm really sorry, Chloe and Zoey, but as a surprise, I tried to buy tickets to the Sweetheart Dance for you both, but they were sold out"?!

NO WAY!!

Unfortunately, honesty, integrity and maturity are NOT my strong points.

So instead, I decided to just fake it by giving them some junk from my locker. . .

SURPRISE! CHLOE AND ZOEY, AS A TOKEN
OF HOW MUCH I CHERISH OUR FRIENDSHIP,
I'D LIKE TO GIVE YOU THIS PACK OF
TISSUES AND TUBE OF LIP GLOSS,
BOTH ONLY SLIGHTLY USED!

Of course, they both thought I was nuts. They
looked at me, and then at their 'surprise', and then
at each other, and then back at me, and then at
their 'surprise' again, and then at each other.

Finally Zoey forced a smile and said, "Nikki! Um,
thanks. You . . . shouldn't have!"

79

But Chloe was NOT having it. "Yeah, Nikki. She's right! You really SHOULDN'T have! You're kidding, right?! Please tell me this isn't the big surprise you were telling us abo—" That's when Zoey gave Chloe a swift kick in the shin to shut her up.

"We totally love our gifts! Right, Chloe?" Zoey said, glaring at Chloe through a fake smile.

"I'll love them if it will keep you from KICKING me again!" Chloe grumbled under her breath, still rubbing her shin.

I plastered a fake smile across my face. "Um, you're both welcome! ENJOY!"

And YES! I was a total loser for tricking my friends like that.

And now I'm feeling REALLY guilty.

I can't believe I actually gave my BFFs slightly used TISSUE pack and LIP GLOSS!!

I mean, WHO does THAT?!

I'm such a TOTAL LOSER!

I wouldn't even want to be FRIENDS with MYSELF ☹!

Unfortunately, my day didn't get any better.

Once I got home, there was even more bad news waiting for me.

Trevor Chase had called and said he needed to reschedule for next month. He's in the process of producing a television special for Lady Gaga and was going to be in New York City for another three weeks.

So now my band and I WON'T be meeting with him on Saturday to discuss recording our original song.

My exciting career as a filthy-rich, world-famous POP STAR was over before it had even gotten started.

That's showbiz!

☹!!

I was a little worried when I saw a note from Chloe
and Zoey on my locker this morning. . .

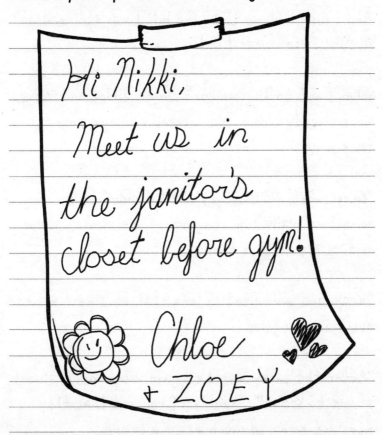

Hi Nikki,

Meet us in
the janitor's
closet before gym!

Chloe
+ ZOEY

After giving them those crazy "gifts" yesterday,
I figured they had decided that I was WAY too
FLAKY to be their friend.

They were probably mad at me and demanding both an explanation and an apology for my bizarre behaviour yesterday.

And I didn't blame them one bit. I was still mad at MYSELF for what I did.

When I got to the janitor's closet, Chloe and Zoey were already there. But instead of being angry, they were SUPERexcited about something.

"Guess what, Nikki! Zoey and I decided to do something really fun. It's kind of a surprise!" Chloe said, giving me jazz hands.

"Yeah, and we waited so long that we almost missed out!" Zoey giggled.

"After the tacky surprise I gave you two, I'm almost afraid to see it!" I said, very relieved that they were not going to ditch me as a friend.

"Okay, now close your eyes!" Chloe said. And then they both shouted . . .

"SURPRISE!!"

When I opened my eyes, I was half expecting them to dump a bucket of water on me as a prank to repay me for those tacky gifts.

Then I noticed they were holding something in their hands . . .

TICKETS TO THE SWEETHEART DANCE ☺!!

My mouth dropped open. "OMG! Chloe! Zoey! You guys have tickets to the dance?! You BOTH decided to go? I'm SOOO happy for you!" I gushed. "Yesterday I tried to buy six tickets for us too. But they were sold out! That was actually going to be my REAL surprise!"

However, deep down I felt a little sad, because I really wanted all of us to go to the dance together. Our romantic dream of going on a triple date would have FINALLY come true!

But it wasn't like I was jealous of them or anything. I mean, how juvenile would THAT be?!

"Wow! YOU actually tried to buy tickets for US?!" Zoey exclaimed. "Well, Nikki. . ."

WE BOUGHT TICKETS FOR YOU!!

OMG! I was SO shocked and surprised when they both handed me my very own tickets to the Sweetheart Dance.

Chloe had already asked Marcus and he said YES!
And Zoey had already asked Theo and he said YES!

So now I just have to get up enough nerve to ask
Brandon! And PRAY he hasn't ALREADY agreed to
go with MacKenzie.

I have to admit, I've been giving him a hard time.
And every time he's tried to explain what happened
or apologise, I've pretty much shot him down. But
it's mostly because I'm really frustrated that things
aren't working out the way I had hoped they would.

So on Monday I plan to make the extra effort to
try and patch things up between us.

The Sweetheart Dance is going to be AWESOME!
And Chloe and Zoey are the best friends EVER!

SQUEEEEEEE!!! ☺!!

I had just got home from school when I got another
text message from Brandon. . .

* * * * *

FROM BRANDON:

Busy at Fuzzy Friends bathing a smelly, long-haired dog and thought about you ☺.

4:57 p.m.

* * * * *

Okay, I'm really happy that Brandon was thinking about me and all. But do I really remind him of a smelly, long-haired dog?!!!

* * * * *

FROM NIKKI:

Hi Brandon. Thanks! I think . . .

4:59 p.m.

* * * * *

GRRRRRR!!

OMG!! Did I just growl like a DOG?!

I have to admit, Brandon always seems to be superbusy lately.

If it's not Fuzzy Friends, it's the newspaper or some big photography project.

It's like he doesn't have time for me anymore.

I grabbed my backpack and pulled out that magazine article, "How to Know if a Guy Is Just *NOT* Into You!"

And as I had suspected . . .

3. Suddenly he's always too busy to spend any time with you.

It was another match!

I crossed #3 off of the list.

NOT good!

Okay, now I'm starting to worry that our relationship is *DOOMED!*

☹!!

The last thing I wanted to do was take Brianna to the Kandy Kingdom playland at the mall. But Mom had invited some ladies over for her book club and asked a certain someone to take Brianna out so she wouldn't wreak havoc at home.

This "someone" agreed to do it, but his secret plan was to hang out with friends at the bowling alley and dump Brianna at the mall with her poor, unsuspecting older sister.

Of course, I totally lost it and yelled, "DAD, THAT WAS A REALLY JERKY THING TO DO TO ME!! YOU SHOULD BE ASHAMED!" But I just said it inside my head, so no one else heard it but me.

I sat on a bench in front of Kandy Kingdom and tried to write in my diary. I watched Brianna slide down from the castle tower, jump into the moat filled with balls and bounce in the royal dungeon until my eyes glazed over.

OMG! I was SO bored I wanted to grab one of the giant plastic lollipops and knock myself unconscious to put an end to my suffering. . .

BRIANNA

← ME

To make matters worse, the place was decorated with zillions of HEARTS!

Which, unfortunately, reminded me that the Sweetheart Dance was ONLY a week away and I STILL needed to get up the courage to ask Brandon to go.

JUST GREAT ☹!

I was about to go and grab that giant lollipop, when I saw our neighbor lady, Mrs Wallabanger.

"Hello, Nikki, dear!" she said cheerfully. "What a pleasant surprise to see you here! How are your parents?"

"Hi, Mrs Wallabanger. BOTH of my parents are doing fine. How about YOU?"

Mrs Wallabanger's smile quickly faded. "You say they BOTH have the FLU? Goodness gracious!" She shook her head in pity. "I hear there's a nasty bug going around right now."

In spite of her hearing aid, Mrs Wallabanger was still VERY hard of hearing. She usually misunderstood about 90% of everything I said.

So most of the time I just went along with whatever she said and didn't try to correct her. Although she's a bit eccentric and very feisty, she's basically a nice person.

"Well, you tell your mother I'm going to bring over some of my famous chicken soup, all right, dear?"

"Uh . . . okay," I answered awkwardly.

"Oh! And before I forget, I want to introduce you and Brianna to my grandson," she said.

That's when I noticed the cutest little boy standing behind her. He was about the same age as Brianna.

He saw me looking at him and bashfully hid his face. . .

MRS WALLABANGER, INTRODUCING
ME TO HER GRANDSON

"Brianna!" I motioned for her to join us. "Come say hello to Mrs Wallabanger's grandson."

"What grandson?" she asked, looking around. "Is he invisible?"

"Girls, I want you to meet Oliver," Mrs Wallabanger said. "Don't be shy, Oliver. Nikki and Brianna won't bite."

I grabbed Brianna firmly by her shoulders. I don't bite. But with her, you can never be too careful. Oliver saw Brianna and came out of hiding.

"Hi there, Mrs Wallabanger's grandson!" Brianna said excitedly. She gave him a toothy grin and held out her hand to shake his.

But he just looked at her and stared at her hand in amazement. Suddenly he pulled something out of his pocket and placed it over his hand. It was a tattered gym sock. It had several small holes and was covered with dirt stains.

An oversized pair of googly eyes had been sewn onto the sock, and a large button nose was dangling by a loose thread.

"I'm Oliver, and my friend Mr Buttons thinks your hand smells like Cheetos," he said, holding up his sock puppet.

"That's 'cause Miss Penelope and me had some for lunch," she replied, and licked sticky orange dust from her fingers. "Mmm . . . cheesy! Wanna taste?"

She shoved her slobbery hand in Oliver's face.

"GROSS!" He wrinkled his nose and pushed her hand away. "GIRLS GOT COOTIES!"

"Well, you have way more cooties than me, you BIG MEANIE!" Brianna yelled back.

Mrs Wallabanger looked totally confused.

"Now, what's all of this talk about GIRL SCOUT COOKIES and BEANS-'N'-WEENIES?"

"Um, actually, Oliver and Brianna were just having a, um, friendly little discussion about their favourite foods," I lied.

"Well, Nikki, dear, could I ask you to do me a big favour? I'd like to make a quick stop by RadioShack to see if they have some hearing-aid batteries. I like to keep a few extra on hand because without them I can't hear a thing. Would you mind watching Oliver until I return?"

"Sure," I answered. "Just take your time. Brianna and Oliver can get to know each other better."

"Thank you. You're such a sweetheart!" She smiled and pinched my cheek. "I'll be back in two shakes of a lamb's tail."

"Brianna, be nice to Oliver, okay?" I said. "Why don't you two go play together?"

"I don't wanna play with that weirdo!" she shouted. "Look! He has a puppet on his hand! Besides, Miss Penelope's my best friend, and I only play with HER!"

"Well, I don't want to play with YOU, either!" Oliver huffed. "Mr Buttons is the bestest, smartest friend in the world! And he's an astronaut, too!"

"Well, Miss Penelope is a superhero like Princess Sugar Plum. And she keeps the world safe from the evil tooth fairy!" Brianna bragged.

Oliver's eyes widened, and he looked like he'd just seen a ghost.

"Did you just say the t-t-tooth fairy?!" he stammered. "Once I swallowed my tooth so she wouldn't come after me. That fairy lady is CRAZY!"

"You did that TOO?!" Brianna asked in surprise.

The two of them chatted on and on about the tooth fairy, dinosaurs, Princess Sugar Plum and chocolate cake for what seemed like forever.

And get THIS!

Pretty soon Miss Penelope and Mr Buttons joined in on their very weird conversation.

The four of them were acting just like BFFs!

OLIVER, BRIANNA, MR BUTTONS AND MISS
PENELOPE, HAVING A FRIENDLY CHAT TOGETHER

All of the giggling and puppy love was utterly adorable!
Even though it involved two VERY weird little kids.
And their even weirder talking hand puppets.

If they started having play dates together on a regular basis, I'd have obnoxious imaginary friends, migraines, broken furniture, kitchen fires and nervous breakdowns TIMES TWO! No . . . FOUR! I broke into a cold sweat just thinking about it.

"I'm back!" Mrs Wallabanger announced. "It was so kind of you to watch my grandson for me. Enjoy the rest of your day, girls. Now come along, Oliver."

Oliver ran up to his grandmother and took her hand.

"Bye, Miss Penelope!" ~~Oliver~~ Mr Buttons yelled as Oliver waved his little sock-puppet hand.

"Bye, Mr Buttons!" ~~Brianna~~ Miss Penelope screeched with her very big mouth.

After Mrs Wallabanger and Oliver left, I gave Brianna an evil grin. . .

"STOP IT OR I'M TELLING MOM!" she yelled at me. She was blushing profusely, and I couldn't stop laughing.

It was SWEET revenge for all of those times Brianna had embarrassed ME in front of Brandon!

"If I didn't know better, I'd say somebody is having her first crush!" I teased.

"Not me!" Brianna snapped. "But Miss Penelope might like Mr Buttons a teeny-weeny bit because they both love chocolate cake. She told me not to tell anyone, so you have to promise to keep it a secret!"

"Okay. I promise," I said, and gave her a big hug.

So maybe the thought of Brianna having a crush isn't that nauseating.

I'm a romantic, after all.

I can already picture their future wedding. Brianna would be dressed in a designer Princess Sugar Plum gown and Oliver would be wearing a clunky astronaut suit. . .

BRIANNA AND OLIVER'S WEDDING

The "kiddie gourmet" wedding feast would include gummy bear appetizers, spaghetti hoops, chicken nuggets, crackers, Hawaiian Punch, and a five-tiered chocolate cake with bubble-gum filling.

How CUTE would THAT be?

Hey, even little PSYCHOS like Brianna need love too! ☺!

SUNDAY, FEBRUARY 9

I'm already DREADING school tomorrow.

Why?

Because we have a floating skills test in swimming class.

Hey, if a human was meant to float, we'd be made of plastic. And instead of having a belly button we'd have a little nozzle thingy so we could be pumped full of air, just like a tyre. I'm just sayin'!

Whenever I try to swim in the deep end of the pool, I pretty much sink right to the bottom.

Like a really heavy rock.

But that's not the worst part!

Do you have any idea of the very gross stuff that's lying on the bottoms of swimming pools?!

It's like an underwater lost-and-found down there. . .

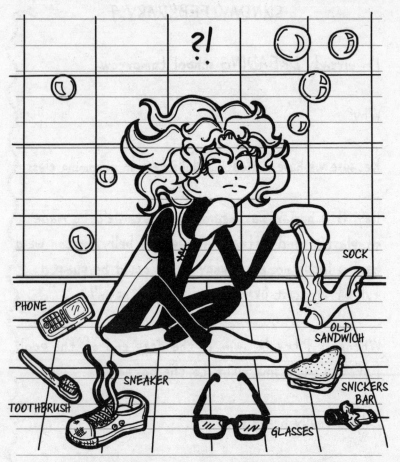

ME, LOOKING AT ALL OF THE JUNK
AT THE BOTTOM OF THE POOL

What I really need is a swimming-class excuse
form that other kids and I can use to get out
of swimming class. . .

SWIMMING-CLASS
EXCUSE FORM

FROM: _____
(YOUR NAME)

TO: _____
(NAME OF SWIMMING INSTRUCTOR)

RE: Medical Excuse for Swimming Class

It is with

- ☐ great sorrow
- ☐ a really bad headache
- ☐ food stuck in my teeth
- ☐ a funky foot odour

that I inform you that I am unable to participate in today's swimming class. Last night I discovered that I'm severely allergic to

- ☐ my mom's meat loaf.
- ☐ my little brother's boogers.
- ☐ most crawling insects.
- ☐ water.

After swallowing just a tiny amount, I became really
- ☐ nervous
- ☐ dizzy
- ☐ constipated
- ☐ confused

and accidentally fell
- ☐ into the bathtub
- ☐ down the stairs
- ☐ in love
- ☐ into a snake pit

and totally busted my
- ☐ liver.
- ☐ tailbone.

☐ nose.

☐ baby toe.

Due to the massive trauma I suffered, I suddenly and unexpectedly went into

☐ a medley of show tunes.

☐ a closet to hide from the tooth fairy.

☐ a fit of involuntary hiccuping.

☐ my sister's room to yell at her.

I was rushed by ambulance to the emergency room, where the doctor told me I was lucky to be alive. Apparently, exposure to the high concentration of

☐ spit

☐ bacteria

☐ disease

☐ belly-button fluff

found in pool water could be deadly and cause both a serious infection and a severe case of

☐ abnormally hairy legs.
☐ irritable bowel syndrome.
☐ compulsive chicken dancing.
☐ projectile vomiting.

Of course I am
☐ totally devastated
☐ surprised and shocked
☐ dazed and confused
☐ completely baffled

by this awful news. As a health precaution,
my doctor has ordered me to avoid pool
water for at least the next
☐ week.
☐ month.
☐ year.
☐ decade.

Thank you for understanding my health
situation and being so amazingly

☐ sympathetic.

☐ ugly.

☐ gullible.

☐ stupid.

Sincerely,

_____

(YOUR SIGNATURE)

Am I NOT brilliant?!!

☺!!

NOTE TO SELF: THE SWEETHEART DANCE IS IN FOUR DAYS ☺!! ASK BRANDON ASAP!

Last night I dug around in the garage and found a big box of Brianna's old water toys that had been put away back when she was a toddler. Hey, I was desperate!

But the good news is that I found the cutest little floating-toy thingy that fit around my waist perfectly.

As long as I didn't try to breathe.

And packed in the same box was a SUPERold swimsuit that belonged to my grandma when she was a little girl.

I thought I looked pretty cute walking out to the pool for swimming class.

Until Chloe gasped, Zoey covered her eyes and everyone else stared.

SIERRA THE SEA HORSE AND I GET
READY FOR MY FLOATING SKILLS TEST.

MacKenzie just looked me up and down like she had never seen a swimsuit with LEGS. Or Sierra, a hot-pink Princess Sugar Plum Baby Sea Horse floating toy with purple hearts on it!

I mean, WHERE has that girl been all of her life?

Under a ROCK?!!

Then MacKenzie batted her eyes at me all innocent-like and made a very snarky and insulting comment in front of the entire class.

"Um, excuse me, Nikki. But the class for Water Babies meets tomorrow at four p.m., NOT today."

Of course everyone snickered.

I could NOT believe that girl had the nerve to publicly insinuate that I was a Water Baby!!

"Gee thanks, MacKenzie, for the info on the other class!" I said really sweetly. "Now why don't you go and jump into the deep end of the pool, swallow twenty-seven gallons of water, and EXPLODE!'"

And of course my gym teacher didn't help matters
any. She said I couldn't get into the pool with
my sea horse because floating toys were NOT
allowed.

But I didn't see that rule posted on the wall. It
only said:

WCD POOL RULES

1. NO running!

2. NO eating!

3. NO horseplay!

4. NO peeing in the pool!

Anyway, I must have had a really big breakfast or
something, because when I tried to take it off,
that stupid sea horse was STUCK! Even Chloe
and Zoey couldn't pry it off of me. . .

CHLOE AND ZOEY, TRYING TO HELP
ME GET OUT OF THAT SEA HORSE

And because I could hardly breathe I started having
these really WEIRD hallucinations. I saw myself:

In bio class sitting next to Brandon while wearing
the sea horse.

Going to the Sweetheart Dance wearing the sea horse.

Graduating from high school wearing the sea horse.

Moving into my college dormitory wearing the sea horse.

Getting married wearing the sea horse.

And giving birth to my first child wearing the sea horse.

OMG! It was like I was going to be STUCK wearing the sea horse the rest of MY LIFE!

That's when I just totally lost it and started SCREAMING hysterically!

Or due to a lack of oxygen, maybe I was just HALLUCINATING that I was screaming hysterically. I really couldn't tell for sure since I was very confused.

That's when my gym teacher called the janitor and told him to come ASAP because she had an emergency situation.

He actually had to cut the sea horse thingy off of

me with these giant metal clippers. Which of course made me supernervous.

One little accidental SNIP and I could have lost an arm or leg or something.

Hey, it could happen! I'd ALREADY lost a braid to Brianna just eight days ago.

Anyway, the good news is that after the janitor finally got that thing off, I started breathing again.

OMG! I felt SO much better after that sea horse fiasco was over!

But the surprising thing was that my gym teacher actually gave me a passing score on my floating skills testing for "Good effort!" Mainly because she said she'd had enough DRAMA for one day and DIDN'T want me in the pool endangering MY life, HER life, or the lives of other STUDENTS in the class.

I was SUPERhappy things turned out so well! ☺!

Anyway, I still had to figure out how I was going to ask Brandon to the Sweetheart Dance.

I had no idea how all of the other girls at my school were brave enough to ask their crushes to the dance.

I guess the major difference is that I'm a spineless coward and just the thought of Brandon possibly saying no totally freaked me out.

I decided to take the direct approach: Track him down in the newspaper office. And just . . . ASK him.

I mean, how hard could it be?

EXTREMELY ☹!!

I had a dry mouth, shaky knees, and a stomach full of rabid butterflies.

And that was from just merely thinking about it.

But apparently, Brandon and the rest of our photography staff were on a two-day field trip touring a local community newspaper. So my only option is to talk to him about the dance when he returns on Wednesday.

I STILL can't believe I actually passed my floating skills test!

WOO-HOO!

☺!!

NOTE TO SELF: THE SWEETHEART DANCE IS
IN THREE DAYS ☺!!

I just LOATHE shopping for Valentine's cards with
Brianna. It's the same DRAMA every single year.

"But I just gotta have the Princess Sugar Plum
valteen cards!" Brianna whined.

Mom had dropped Brianna and me off at the main
entrance of the mall while she hunted for a parking space.

"It's V-A-L-E-N-T-I-N-E! Not valteen!" I
grumbled.

"If I don't get my Princess Sugar Plum cards, I will
cry once upon a time in a faraway land, forever and
ever, the end!" she whimpered.

"Well, unless you want me to drop you off at the
mall's lost and found, you'd better NOT cry forever
and ever!" I muttered.

"ACTUALLY, I *FOUND* THIS LITTLE GIRL
THROWING A TANTRUM IN THE MALL. . . ."

"Anyway, it's just a silly card that kids in your class will throw away the second they open it! So what's the big deal?!" I grumped.

"I want my Princess Sugar Plum valteens! NOW!" Brianna cried.

We searched for those cruddy Princess Sugar Plum valentines all afternoon. And nine stores, five tantrums and one migraine headache later, we STILL hadn't found any. Every single store was sold out!

At least the mall was prepared for the onslaught. Sales clerks at every store were strategically stationed by their Valentine's display holding boxes of tissues for the kids who burst into tears once they found out that the Princess Sugar Plum Valentine's Day cards were all sold out.

It was totally disgusting how most of the stores had taken complete advantage of the situation and set up huge displays with other Princess Sugar Plum products. . .

It was quite obvious they were hoping the traumatised little brats would buy an assortment of the forty-nine other Princess Sugar Plum products instead.

There was Princess Sugar Plum bubble bath, body lotion, shampoo, toothpaste, vitamins, Band-Aids, sweets, pretend glitter makeup, bubble gum, cereal, breakfast bars, peanut butter, dolls, board games, fashions, dog food etc.

Basically, you name it, they had it.

Somewhere on a remote island there's probably a secret factory where fat little purple elves with pointy little shoes, sugar plum hair and creepy, beady little eyes crank out Princess Sugar Plum junk twenty-four hours a day, seven days a week. Kind of like that Willie Wonka guy and his chocolate factory.

Of course, when Brianna didn't find the Princess Sugar Plum valentines, she quickly morphed into a wailing, slobbering, snot-nosed wreck.

But what I couldn't figure out was how the sales clerks could be so calm and peaceful in the midst of total chaos!

There were little girls crying, screaming, yelling, screeching, shrieking and squealing everywhere.

How could they just stand there smiling calmly through all of that high-pitched, eardrum-shattering noise while a couple of hundred five-year-olds threw simultaneous tantrums?

I was impressed.

Until I saw their secret weapon.

EARPLUGS!!!

Yes!

Those SNEAKY little scoundrels!!

The clerks were all wearing earplugs to protect their hearing AND their sanity!!

Anyway, Mom and I were exhausted from shopping, and Brianna was an emotional basket case.

In the car on the way home I came up with a BRILLIANT idea!

"Brianna, what do you think about me making your Princess Sugar Plum valentines instead? I'm a pretty decent artist, and I'm sure you'd love 'em."

Brianna immediately stopped crying and looked at me suspiciously, like I was trying to sell her some swampland in Florida — really cheap!

"But if YOU make them, they won't be REAL Princess Sugar Plum valteen cards!" she sulked.

That's when Mom winked at me. "Brianna, dear, I have a wonderful idea! How about while Nikki is making your cards, you can eat a big, yummy bowl of Princess Sugar Plum cereal for dinner?!"

Brianna's eyes lit up. "Princess Sugar Plum cereal! FOR DINNER?! THAT would be FUN!" She giggled.

But suddenly Brianna's mood darkened and she started to pout again.

"But, Moooom! I just ate the last booowl of Princess Sugar Plum cereal this morning. And we don't have any more miiiilk," she cried pitifully.

Mom quickly spun the car around by doing a U-turn right in the middle of the street as I held on for dear life. SCREEEEECH!! (That was our tyres!)

"Then we'll just stop at the grocery store and you and Nikki can run in and get some cereal and milk! How does that sound?" Mom asked cheerfully.

"Well . . . okay, I g-guess." Brianna sniffed glumly.

Once we were inside the store, I held Brianna's hand so she wouldn't wander off or get into any trouble. Then we headed for the cereal aisle.

"Hmmm! Let's see. . ." I muttered to myself as I tapped my chin. "Princess Sugar Plum cereal with tooty-fruity marshmallows, Princess Sugar Plum cereal with princess fairy dust, Princess Sugar Plum cereal with glitter sprinkles, and finally, Princess Sugar Plum cereal with a free mini glow-in-the-dark tiara. . ."

ME →

ME, TRYING TO FIGURE OUT WHICH CEREAL
TO BUY WHILE WATCHING BRIANNA (SORT OF)

There were so many choices I couldn't make up my mind. "Brianna, which cereal do you want?" I asked as I turned around.

That's when I discovered she had disappeared into thin air!

Although, it WASN'T the first time. I broke into a cold sweat as memories of the time I lost Brianna at the *Nutcracker* ballet flooded into my brain.

"*NOOOOO!!!* Not *AGAIN!*" I shrieked as I frantically ran down the aisle. "BRIANNA. . .!!"

Suddenly I spotted her!

She had stacked a pile of assorted grocery items on the floor and climbed up on top of them.

Then, balancing dangerously on her tippy toes, she was reaching desperately for an item on the top shelf of a big colourful display. This is what happened. . .

135

Well, there was good news and bad news.

The good news was that Brianna wasn't hurt.

The bad news was that it felt like I had busted my spleen or something.

Or maybe it was just that Brianna had kicked me in my gut with her chunky Princess Sugar Plum snow boot when she landed on top of me.

In any event, the annual quest to find Princess Sugar Plum valentines was finally over.

And I had managed to survive yet another year.

With ONLY a busted spleen.

Woo-hoo!

☺!

NOTE TO SELF: THE DANCE IS IN TWO DAYS ☺!!
ASK BRANDON!! IT'S NOW OR NEVER!!

Today everyone was buzzing about who was going to
be crowned Sweetheart Princess.

Students can vote for any eighth-grade girl.
However, the girls who wanted it really badly (like
MacKenzie) were putting up posters. The entire
student body votes during school on February 14,
and the winner will be announced later that night
at the dance.

According to the latest gossip, everyone was
pretty sure MacKenzie was going to win. Especially
MacKenzie!

OMG! That girl is so hopelessly VAIN!

All day she was acting supernice to everyone and
giving out sweet hearts and free fashion advice to
bribe people to vote for her.

Although, I have to admit, her posters are
SUPERCUTE. . . !

MACKENZIE'S
SUPERCUTE →
POSTERS

I ALMOST wanted to vote for her MYSELF!
NOT! ☺!!

Anyway, TODAY was the big day!

During bio I was FINALLY going to ask Brandon to
go to the Sweetheart Dance with me.

OMG! I was a nervous wreck!

And yes! I realised there was a possibility he might
already be going with MacKenzie. But at this point I
had nothing to lose.

I gulped down my lunch. Then I rushed to the girls'
bathroom and practised what I was going to say to
him in the mirror . . .

"Brandon, I know this is kind of last-minute and
everything, but I would really love it if you would
take me to the Sweetheart Dance!"

In the bathroom, everything went PERFECTLY!

But when I actually tried to ask Brandon, I got totally distracted by all of the stuff that was going on in class. . .

. . . A POP QUIZ??!!
OKAY, CLASS! PLEASE TAKE OUT A PIECE OF PAPER AND DIAGRAM THE KREBS CYCLE!
ACTUALLY, NIKKI, I HATE POP QUIZZES! BUT I GUESS TODAY'S YOUR LUCKY DAY!
Today! Pop Quiz Krebs Cycle

OMG! That quiz was a complete DISASTER!! We were supposed to draw the Krebs cycle, and I totally KNEW the correct answer.

However, I was so FREAKED out by the whole asking-Brandon-to-the-Sweetheart-Dance fiasco that I totally blanked out and couldn't remember a thing. So I just drew the first thing that popped into my head...

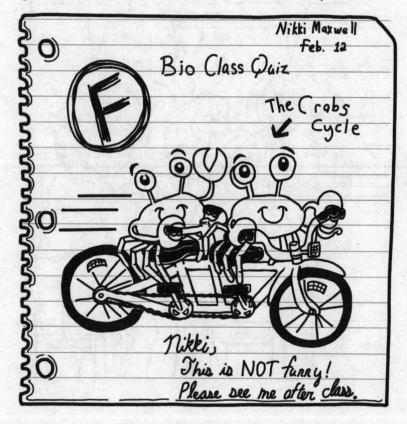

Unfortunately, my teacher did NOT appreciate MY creativity, humour, or artistic talent.

When I talked to Ms Kincaid after class, she told me I was in bio, not ART class. Then she warned me that if I got another grade below a C or goofed-off in her class again, she was sending a note home to my parents.

Of course they would totally overreact and take away my phone AND ground me until my eighteenth birthday.

Thank goodness Ms Kincaid allows us to drop our lowest test score at the end of the semester.

Anyway, I STILL have to ask Brandon to the dance!!

ARRGHH!!!

That was me pulling my hair out in frustration.

Why is my life so massively CRUDDY?!

!!

Yesterday I was so upset about Brandon and that stupid bio quiz that I planned to go straight to my room and have myself a big pity party.

Brianna was in the kitchen humming to herself and working on her Princess Sugar Plum ~~valteen~~ cards. . .

That's when the most FABULOUS idea popped into my head!

I had totally embarrassed myself trying to ask Brandon to the Sweetheart Dance.

But what if I gave him a Valentine's Day card instead?

Then I could WRITE a little note inside inviting him to the Sweetheart Dance!!

It would be cute, sweet, and romantic!

SQUEEE ☺!

How could he say no to that?!!

I scavenged the house for cool stuff I could use for his card and found glitter, satin ribbon, red foil wrapping paper, lace, rhinestones and gel pens.

Then, blasting my favourite Taylor Swift tunes for inspiration, I created a beautiful, one-of-a-kind, personalised valentine just for Brandon. . .

ME, MAKING A CARD FOR BRANDON

The final step was to write a deep, heartfelt poem inspired by our friendship and mutual respect for each other. Like . . .

ROSES ARE RED,
VIOLETS ARE BLUE,
I'D REALLY LOVE TO GO
TO THE SWEETHEART
DANCE WITH
YOU!!

Yes, I know!

My poem is cheesier than two large pizzas.

Taylor Swift makes writing mushy songs about your boyfriend look really easy.

Anyway, this morning I went to school ten minutes early so I could give Brandon my card before classes started.

But it wasn't until second period that I FINALLY spotted him at his locker talking to Theo!

I didn't have a choice but to go into stalker mode and secretly follow him around, waiting for the perfect moment to give him the card.

But that moment NEVER came. Someone was always hanging around or talking to him. I didn't know the guy was so popular.

Although I was still pretty traumatised from that pop quiz fiasco yesterday, one thing was very clear. Cornering Brandon in bio class was going to be my ONLY chance at attending the Sweetheart Dance!

I got to class superearly and just sat there clutching my card, waiting for him to arrive. I was a nervous wreck!

And having the extra time to think just made me worry about all of the things that could go wrong AFTER he read my poem.

I mean, what if Brandon said NO? Or laughed at me? Or just . . . PUKED?!

OMG! I was a sweaty, paranoid . . . WRECK! I felt like people were staring at me and whispering about me. . .

ME, NERVOUSLY WAITING FOR BRANDON
SO I COULD GIVE HIM MY CARD

When Brandon finally arrived, I thought I was going
to pee my pants.

"What's up, Nikki?!" he said, brushing his hair out of his eyes and giving me a crooked smile.

I just stared at him. I opened my mouth to say hi, but no words came out.

"Um . . . are you okay?" he suddenly asked, looking concerned. "You look a little, um . . . frazzled!"

"Actually, Brandon . . ." I finally blurted out really loud, "I just wanted to give—"

"BRAAAN-DON! Wasn't that pop quiz yesterday just AWFUL?" MacKenzie asked, rudely interrupting me. "I thought I failed for sure. But lucky for me I squeaked by with a B+. So, Nikki, what did YOU get on the quiz, hon?"

Then she smiled at me and batted her eyes all innocent-like.

I wanted to slap that smile right off her face.

But before I could answer, MacKenzie turned her

back to me and started gushing to Brandon about how much she was looking forward to seeing all of the great photos he'd taken with that new camera she'd given him for his birthday.

I could NOT believe that girl was ignoring me right to my face like that. And get this! She kept blabbing her big fat mouth right up until our teacher arrived.

Which totally RUINED my chance to talk to Brandon BEFORE class. And if MacKenzie had her way, she'd HOG all of his attention and totally RUIN my chance to talk to him AFTER class TOO!

I was sick and tired of her little mind games.

So that's when I decided I'd just give Brandon my card DURING class! Hey, I sat right next to him!

And MacKenzie couldn't do a thing to stop me.

Because our class had performed poorly on our pop

quiz yesterday, Ms Kincaid planned to spend the entire hour at the board diagramming the Krebs cycle while we took notes.

OMG! Her lecture was SO boring I thought my brain was going to melt and ooze out of my ears. . .

"The citric acid cycle — also known as the Krebs cycle — is a series of chemical reactions used by all aerobic organisms to generate energy through the oxidisation of acetate derived from carbohydrates, fats and proteins into carbon dioxide. In addition . . ."

I stared at Brandon for what seemed like FOREVER waiting for him to look in my direction. But he was busy taking notes.

That's when I took my pencil and gently poked his arm.

At first he looked slightly startled, then a little confused.

I pulled the card out of my notebook and mouthed the words "For YOU!"

He blinked in surprise and then pointed at himself, as if to say "For ME?!"

I nodded my head. "Yes!"

As I watched Ms Kincaid out of the corner of my eye, I quickly shoved the card in Brandon's direction.

However, I think that supercute smile of his must have affected my nervous system and messed up my hand-eye coordination or something. Because the valentine slid right past him, glided across the floor, and landed centimetres from Ms Kincaid's left foot!

I wanted to jump out of my seat and try to grab it before she saw it.

But someone right behind me started to cough.

Really loudly.

And because it was such an obviously FAKE cough, I guessed that it was MacKenzie.

Distracted by the noise, Ms Kincaid turned around.

I pretended not to notice the big glittery red valentine lying on the floor right in front of her. But it didn't matter because everyone else in the room was staring at it like it was a four-metre-long two-headed flesh-eating snake.

"Okay, people. I'm up here trying to teach you this stuff! And someone has decided to disrupt the class by handing out valentines a day early?!!"

Everyone snickered.

"So, who does THIS belong to?" she asked as she reached down and picked up the card.

The room was so quiet, you could hear a pin drop. Neither Brandon nor I felt morally obligated to offer a confession.

He kept HIS mouth shut because if I brought the card to class, it belonged to ME (not HIM).

And I kept MY mouth shut because if I'd just given the card away, it technically belonged to HIM (not ME).

Unfortunately, my cover was quickly blown. Probably because the back of the card had big letters that said: "From Nikki" DUH!!

"Miss Maxwell, I think this belongs to you!" Ms Kincaid said, glaring at me.

"Um, it kind of fell out of my notebook. Accidentally," I muttered.

"Really? So you weren't passing notes in class?"

"Actually, I wouldn't really call it a note?" I mumbled. "It's more of a . . . card."

The class snickered again.

"Actually, I—I was hoping you wouldn't share it with the class?" I stammered.

More laughter. OMG! I was SO embarrassed. I wanted to dig a really deep hole right in the middle of the floor, crawl into it, and . . . DIE!

Brandon's cheeks were flushed, and he looked really nervous.

Ms Kincaid read the card silently, crossed her arms and stared at me.

Then, choosing to spare Brandon the massive embarrassment, she turned, marched across the room and tossed my valentine onto her desk.

"Nikki, please see me after class!"

I could feel everyone's eyes on me. MacKenzie, now miraculously cured from her coughing affliction, had this smug little look on her face.

Brandon shrugged and mouthed the word "Sorry!"

But I just stared blankly straight ahead.

I could NOT believe that MacKenzie had totally set me up! AGAIN!! I was so mad I could SPIT!!

And now I was going to get a note sent home to my parents and possibly even an after-school detention.

Finally the bell rang and bio was over.

Brandon actually looked kind of upset. "I'm really sorry about what happened, Nikki! I'll just wait for you right outside the door until you're done talking to the teacher, okay?"

"Don't worry! It was just a stupid card. I'll be fine. Really!" I said, trying to muster a smile. "The last thing you need is a tardy."

"I guess you're right. I just feel bad since you made that card for me." Suddenly his face brightened. "Hey! I'm going to hang out at Fuzzy Friends after school today. The bakery across the street makes some mean cupcakes! Why don't you stop by? It'll be my treat! Besides, we haven't really talked much since my birthday."

"Yeah, that would be very cool, actually!" I blushed.

"But I'm supposed to watch Brianna after school today. I'll text my mom and ask if I—"

"MISS MAXWELL!" Ms Kincaid interrupted. "Whenever you're done chatting, I'll be here WAITING . . . !"

"Sorry!" I said to Brandon, rolling my eyes. "I'll see you later. Maybe."

"Later. Hopefully!" Brandon smiled and gave me a thumbs-up. Then he headed for the door.

I shoved all of my stuff into my backpack and slowly walked up to my teacher's desk.

"Um, you wanted to see me?" I muttered. I was expecting the worst.

"Nikki, I've noticed you've been really distracted lately. Yesterday you drew a cartoon on your quiz and today you were disrupting class by giving out valentines instead of taking notes. Is everything okay?"

I shrugged my shoulders. "I'm okay, I guess. It's just that the Sweetheart Dance is tomorrow. I planned to ask Brandon yesterday, but we had that pop quiz. Then today you confiscated my card before I could give it to him. So things are just . . . cruddy!" I explained, trying to ignore the large lump in my throat.

Suddenly Ms Kincaid smiled and shook her head.

"When I was your age, I thought I'd NEVER survive middle school! But I did, and so will YOU. Here!" she said, handing my valentine back to me. Then she winked at me. "Good luck!"

I just stared at her with my mouth open. I was so shocked, I didn't know what to say.

"Thank you! I can't believe you just . . . ! Thank you!" I sputtered.

"Now, I'm warning you, Miss Maxwell. No more funny business in my class, or you're going to be doodling crabs AND giving out valentines in DETENTION."

I did my Snoopy "happy dance" all the way to the library. Inside my head!

My Plan A had failed. But now I had a Plan B!

I would meet Brandon at Fuzzy Friends after school. Then, while we shared a yummy cupcake, I'd give him my valentine.

SQUEEE ☺!!

He'd say YES! And by this time tomorrow my BFFs and I would be just hours away from our very first dates.

A triple date! Just like we'd dreamed of!

I texted my mom, and she said I could hang out at Fuzzy Friends, but only for forty-five minutes since it was a school night and I had homework.

Finally school was over! It was hard to believe that in just ten minutes it was going to be official.

I'd actually be going to the Sweetheart Dance with Brandon! SQUEEE ☺!!

I was at my locker getting my coat when I got two texts barely a minute apart. I thought they were from my mom. But I was pleasantly surprised to see that they were from . . . BRANDON!

However, I gasped in shock when I read them . . .

* * * * *

FROM BRANDON:

Hey MacKenzie,

What's up! Wasn't bio crazy today?

3:07 p.m.

* * * * *

FROM BRANDON:

Sorry, Nikki! My bad. Wrong #.

3:08 p.m.

* * * * *

OMG! I had a meltdown right there at my locker!

HOW COULD BRANDON

ACCIDENTALLY SEND A TEXT

MEANT FOR MACKENZIE TO ME?!!

I don't know if I was more angry or disgusted!
It seemed like Brandon was ALWAYS talking to
MacKenzie or working on some random newspaper
project with her.

And now it was quite obvious he was TEXTING her on a pretty regular basis too!

All while inviting ME to hang out at Fuzzy Friends and eat cupcakes with him??!! I mean, WHO does that?!!

I reached into my backpack and dug out that wrinkled magazine article, "How to Know if a Guy Is Just NOT Into You."

I read it over, then crossed off the last item left on the list:

5. He's spending way too much time with another girl.

I sighed and blinked back my tears. I felt so STUPID!

Brandon was NOT interested in me at all.

And according to the EXPERTS, he'd done all FIVE of the things on the magazine checklist! I'd carefully documented each and every one. . .

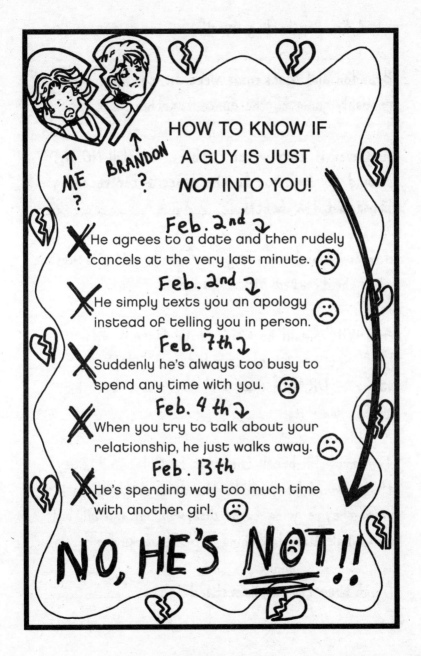

I had to stop fooling myself.

Brandon and MacKenzie were an item and were probably going to the dance together.

And even if they weren't, there was still NO WAY I could ask Brandon to the dance after receiving those last two texts!

How could he be really good friends with MacKenzie when she treated ME so badly?

And WHY would he want to be friends with her?! She was a mean, spoiled, manipulative, vain . . . DRAMA QUEEN! And those were her BEST qualities!

Tomorrow I'll break the news to Chloe and Zoey that I won't be going to the dance with them. I know they're going to be disappointed and all, but this whole Brandon thing is NOT working out.

I just hope they'll understand.

It's really sad losing a good friend like Brandon to MacKenzie. And the last thing I want is to lose my BFFs, too.

Then I'd be all alone at this school again.

I sighed deeply and slammed my locker door shut just as MacKenzie and Jessica brushed past me, giggling.

"OMG! Jess!" MacKenzie gushed. "Guess who just texted me?!"

She showed her phone to Jessica. Then they both squealed in excitement like two baby pigs or something.

I didn't want to fight with MacKenzie.

I didn't want to go to the dance with Brandon.

I didn't want to disappoint my BFFs.

All I REALLY wanted to do was rush home and have a really good CRY!

But first I had to stop by the girls' bathroom.

Only, it wasn't for the most obvious reason.

I sniffed and wiped away a tear that had trickled down my cheek.

Then I ripped Brandon's valentine into tiny pieces and flushed it down the toilet!

I had pretty much accepted the fact that I WASN'T going to the Sweetheart Dance. But I still felt disappointed, hurt and just plain miserable.

I must have been pretty traumatised by the whole thing, because I had the most horrible nightmare!

It was the night of the Sweetheart Dance, and I was at home putting dishes in the dishwasher and feeling kind of depressed about my life.

Suddenly my fairy godmother appeared and waved her magic wand. She turned my heart pj's into a beautiful evening gown and my bunny slippers into glass slippers.

Then she waved her wand again and turned Brianna's Princess Sugar Plum Magical Flying Car (with real working headlights) into a life-size limo and Brianna's Baby Unicorn into a chauffeur.

OMG! It was like I was Cinderella or someone!

And when I arrived at the Sweetheart Dance, Brandon was dressed like a prince and standing there waiting for me. We danced the night away and had a wonderful time together. It was SO romantic!

Then, at the stroke of midnight, MacKenzie was crowned Sweetheart Princess and my fairy tale turned into a horror story.

My gown and glass slippers turned back into my pj's and bunny slippers. And my limo and chauffeur turned back into the Princess Sugar Plum Magical Flying Car (with real working headlights) and Baby Unicorn.

OMG! I was SO embarrassed to be at the school dance in my pajamas with Brianna's toys. Everyone was laughing at me. Even Brandon, Chloe and Zoey!

But this was the really scary part. Suddenly MacKenzie turned into this huge monster with pointy teeth, and she started growling and chasing me around the dance. I barely escaped by galloping away on Baby Unicorn. . .

GRRRRR!

← MACKENZIE

It was probably the WORST nightmare I'd ever had in my entire life.

I woke up in a cold sweat.

But this is the crazy part!

Even though I was wide awake and staring at the ceiling, I could still hear MacKenzie (or something) growling.

GRRRRRRRRRRRRRR!

GRRRRRRRRRRRRRRR!

GRRRRRRRRRRRRRRR!

And it seemed to be coming from outside.

I rushed to my bedroom window and cautiously peeked out, half expecting to see a glammed-up monster in a tiara terrorising the neighbourhood.

OMG! I couldn't believe my eyes. . .

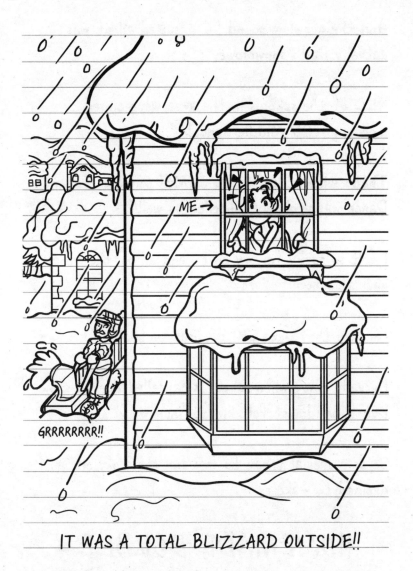

IT WAS A TOTAL BLIZZARD OUTSIDE!!

Overnight, we'd had a whopping tweny centimetres of snow!!

And the growling sound I'd dreamed about was actually Dad's snowblower.

ALL of the schools in the area were closed, including WCD Middle School.

That's when it hit me. . . . OMG! Our Sweetheart Dance was probably cancelled as well!!

I felt so sorry for my BFFs and all of the other girls at school.

I'm sure they were SUPERdisappointed!

I usually enjoy when school is cancelled due to snow. But today I just felt kind of numb.

So as a special treat to try and cheer myself up, I decided to make . . .

HOMEMADE DOUBLE-CHOCOLATE FUDGE ☺ . . . !

BRIANNA!! WHY ARE YOUR HANDPRINTS IN MY DOUBLE-CHOCOLATE FUDGE?!

Luckily, I was able to cover up Brianna's handprints by sprinkling those cute little Valentine heart sweets over the top of the fudge.

BTW, I called Chloe and Zoey to get an update on the Sweetheart Dance. They had good news and bad news! The bad news was that the dance had in fact been cancelled due to the snowstorm. However, the good news was that it's rescheduled for Friday, February 28. Of course, they were disappointed since they were all geared up to go to the dance TONIGHT! But I reminded them that the new date is ONLY two weeks away!

Anyway, after lunch Brianna and I gave Mom and Dad their Valentine's Day cards and some of the fudge I'd made. Of course they LOVED everything!

I was a little shocked to receive a goofy text from Brandon: "HAPPY VALENTINE'S DAY!! Sitting here eating your box of chocolates and thinking of you ☺!"

In spite of the blizzard outside, the Category 1 hurricane inside (also known as Brianna) and my very dark and stormy love life, I actually managed to survive Valentine's Day! I just wish I had some magical glue that could fix all of the broken hearts in the world!!

Today I agreed to watch Mrs Wallabanger's adorable little grandson Oliver for a couple of hours while she played bingo at the senior centre.

Okay! I admit I was wrong! I should NOT have teased Brianna about having a crush on Oliver last week.

And I don't blame her for STILL being a little mad at me about that silly K-I-S-S-I-N-G poem.

But I never imagined she'd go hide in a closet and refuse to play with him. Especially after they got along so well when they played together at Kandy Kingdom in the mall.

Trying to coax Brianna out of the closet was a major headache. "Come on, Brianna! Why don't you come out and play with Oliver? It'll be fun!"

Oliver smiled and nodded his head. "Brianna, do you wanna play Princess Sugar Plum Monster Truck?"

Finally Brianna slowly opened the closet door and peeked out.

BRIANNA, PEEKING OUT OF THE CLOSET

I couldn't believe Brianna was acting like such a little drama queen!

She knew good and well that if Oliver wasn't visiting, I'd snatch her butt out of that closet so fast she'd have a permanent wedgie.

Brianna rolled her eyes at me and finally stomped angrily out of the closet.

That little brat didn't appreciate the fact that I'd spent fifteen minutes setting up the family room with assorted toys, games and stuffed animals!

I'd even managed to find some dinosaurs, astronauts and wild animals for Oliver, thanks to Princess Sugar Plum's Journey to Dino Island, Blast-Off Voyage to Mars and Swinging Safari Adventure.

But in spite of a room full of toys, Brianna and Oliver just sat there staring at each other like strangers.

"Hey, Oliver! Look at this cool T. rex!" I said enthusiastically. "ROAR! ROAR!"

"And, Brianna, why don't you show Oliver your Princess Sugar Plum spaceship with real-life blast-off sound effects! ZOOOOOOM!"

"No way!" Brianna grumped. "Boys have COOTIES!"

Oliver looked sad and sighed. Poor kid! I felt really sorry for him. Then Brianna got really personal and started dissing MY babysitting skills.

"Nikki! As a babysitter, you STINK! If Miss Penelope was watching us, we'd have lots of fun!"

"Fine!" I said. "Then let HER do it! She'll see how hard it is to watch a little brat like you."

"Fine!" Brianna yelled at me. "You're . . . FIRED!"

That's when Brianna brought out Miss Penelope.

A smile spread across Oliver's face as he quickly pulled his tattered Mr Buttons sock puppet from his pocket. Within seconds Miss Penelope was showing Mr Buttons Brianna's Princess Sugar Plum spaceship.

"I'm an astronaut, and I've been all over the galaxy! Wanna see my moon dust?" Mr. Buttons asked.

"You actually have REAL moon dust?!!" Miss Penelope exclaimed.

~~Oliver~~ Mr Buttons reached into Oliver's pocket and dumped a small pile of sand and rocks on the floor. . .

MR BUTTONS SHOWS OFF HIS MOON DUST

"COOL!" Miss Penelope gushed in amazement.

I couldn't believe my eyes! Soon Miss Penelope and Mr Buttons were having so much fun laughing, playing, and running around that Brianna and Oliver joined in too.

The ~~two~~ four of them took a trip to Mars and had a conversation in an alien language. Then they hunted for the tooth fairy in the jungle while riding on dinosaurs.

Since Miss Penelope had both of the munchkins under control (Brianna was right, she WAS a pretty good sitter!), I decided to chillax by having a snack and writing in my diary.

Everything was going great until I heard Oliver crying. Apparently, Mr Buttons was missing. Brianna insisted that he had been KIDNAPPED by the tooth fairy!

Oliver was SUPERupset. "I w-want Mr B-Buttons! He's my b-best f-friend!" he wailed.

Soon Brianna and Miss Penelope started to cry too. "Mr Buttons is g-gone f-forever!"

It looks like I'll have to finish this diary entry later. Right now I have a babysitting emergency on my hands!!

I've heard how people can end up emotionally scarred for life simply by losing their favorite security blanket or toy as a little kid.

Which probably explains why a lot of the kids at my middle school are so MESSED UP!

But what am I supposed to do in a situation like this? Call 911 and report a missing dirty sock named Mr. Buttons?!

☹!!

(TO BE CONTINUED . . .)

Now, where was I (tapping chin and thinking) . . . ?

Okay . . . Mr Buttons was missing! And Oliver, Brianna and Miss Penelope were having a simultaneous meltdown.

We looked EVERYWHERE! And still couldn't find that stupid sock. I knew socks had a nasty habit of disappearing in the dryer. But I had no idea how one could just vanish into thin air.

"Nikki! You're the babysitter!" Brianna screamed. "Do something! And do it NOW!"

I was like, Oh. No. She. DIDN'T!! "Really?! So I'M the babysitter now that Mr Buttons is LOST and everyone is CRYING?!" I yelled at Brianna. "Personally, I think this is all Miss Penelope's fault. Tell HER to go find Mr Buttons!"

But since I WAS the mature, responsible older sister, I decided to take matters into my own hands.

After rummaging through my sock drawer, I found an old mismatched sock with ruffles and lace. I grabbed a black marker and drew on a face. Then I stapled on some wool for hair, dabbed on some cherry-red lip gloss, and *BAM!!* A new puppet was born. I called her Maxine. Mainly because she was as UGLY as Max the Roach. (Max is a two-metre-long hideous-looking plastic bug bolted to the top of my dad's bug extermination van.)

Although, with the big hair, long eyelashes, fancy lace and ruffles sock outfit, clueless expression and five thick layers of lip gloss, she bore a striking resemblance to . . . NEVER MIND. I rushed back into the family room to introduce Maxine to Oliver.

"Oliver, please don't cry!" Maxine pleaded in a squeaky voice. "Everything will be okay. I promise!"

"Wh—who are you?" Oliver sniffed.

"I'm Mr Buttons's older sister. My name is Maxine. Nice to meet you!"

MAXINE

"Wow! You're Mr Buttons's SISTER?!" Oliver giggled as he wiped away his tears.

Brianna must have felt a little jealous or something because she just glared at Maxine and frowned. "Um . . . WHY do you have fluff all over your face?" Brianna asked.

"Yeah, and your hair looks funny too," Miss Penelope scoffed, looking her up and down.

"Hey, back off, girlfriend!" Maxine said, rolling her eyes at Miss Penelope. "At least I HAVE hair!"

So, maybe Maxine WAS a little fluffy. Sorry, but I was NOT about to destroy a good pair of socks. And WHY would Miss Penelope get all snotty and insult another puppet when SHE was a puppet too?! Was I the only person who found all of this disturbing, bizarre and a wee bit creepy?

Maxine continued. "I'm here to help you find Mr Buttons. But don't worry about that guy. He's a prankster and he's probably just playing hide-and-seek!"

Oliver's face brightened. "You think so?"

"Don't listen to her!" Brianna fumed. "I think he's been KIDNAPPED by the TOOTH FAIRY!!"

"I have a great idea, Oliver!" ~~Maxine~~ I said. "Why don't you hang out with Maxine while I finish looking for Mr Buttons. Okay?"

"That would be fun!" Oliver giggled.

I handed Maxine to Oliver. Then I went from room to room in search of Mr Buttons. When I returned, Brianna and Oliver had plastered over a dozen Kidnapped, Missing and Wanted posters all over the family room in their desperate attempt to find that puppet.

Brianna was about to tape a poster to a pillow
on the couch when she suddenly gasped in surprise.
"Hey, look! It's Mr Buttons!! The tooth fairy
kidnapped him and stuck him behind this pillow?!"
she exclaimed.

"Mr Buttons! Mr Buttons!" shouted Oliver. "I'm so
glad to see you!"

We all gave Mr Buttons a great big group hug.

Just then the doorbell rang. It was Mrs Wallabanger.

"Hi, Mrs Wallabanger," I said, thankful she hadn't
arrived five minutes earlier.

"Hello, Nikki, dear. How are my little gangbusters
doing?" she asked cheerfully.

"They're GREAT!" I answered. "We played some
games and even went on a BIG make-believe
ADVENTURE!"

Suddenly Mrs Wallabanger frowned.

"What was that?! You think I've gained weight and need to get a wig and dentures?!" she asked, highly insulted.

"NO! Actually, you look beautiful! Just the way you are," I tried to reassure her.

As Oliver was leaving, he gave me a great big hug.

"Nikki! You're the best sitter me and Mr Buttons have ever had!"

"Thanks, Oliver! Both Maxine and I will be looking forward to you visiting again."

He took a few steps down the sidewalk, holding his grandmother's hand. Then he abruptly turned around and raced back to the door to give Brianna a hug too.

"Thanks for finding Mr Buttons," he whispered. "He made this especially for you!"

Oliver reached into his back pocket and handed Brianna a wad of red construction paper.

Brianna unfolded the paper to reveal the most
beautiful crinkled-up, lopsided Valentine's heart I
have ever seen in my entire life . . .

Both Brianna and Miss Penelope had these big goofy
smiles on their faces as they waved goodbye.

"Bye, Oliver! Bye, Mr Buttons! Come back soon!"

AWWWWWWW ☺! That whole scene was so cute and sickeningly sweet, I almost couldn't stand it.

Yes, Oliver was a little weird. And misunderstood. But he was such a good kid! Mrs Wallabanger was lucky to have him as a grandson.

That's when it hit me that Oliver reminded me a lot of, well . . . he-who-shall-remain-nameless.

Anyway, I was really happy that Brianna had found a new friend she had so much in common with.

I just hope Oliver won't change when he gets older. Like, you know . . . some people.

I almost forgot! Speaking of new friends, I now have a roommate . . . MAXINE!!

She's moving in to my sock drawer.

☺!!

Due to the snowstorm on Friday, today was unofficially Valentine's Day at WCD!

Chloe, Zoey and I traded valentines. And I gave them some of my homemade double-chocolate fudge, which they LOVED!

I noticed Brandon staring at me in the hall this morning. It seemed like he wanted to say something, but I just totally ignored him.

And in bio I noticed he had what looked like a valentine or something stuck in his notebook. I assumed it was probably from MacKenzie. Or maybe even FOR MacKenzie.

But I didn't bother to hang around after class to find out. As soon as the bell rang, I grabbed my stuff and ran out of there like my hair was on fire!

And speaking of MacKenzie, I know that girl HATES my GUTS! But never in a million years did I think she would actually stoop so low as to try to DROWN me!

In gym today my teacher announced that we'd be learning about swimming safety and the buddy system.

Okay, I'll admit it. One of my most embarrassing secrets is that I'm NOT a very good swimmer.

Just imagine how cruddy I feel when Brianna is confidently doggy-paddling around in the deep end while I'm nervously wading in the kiddie pool!

Talk about HUMILIATION ☹!

"Okay, class!" our teacher began. "I hope everyone read over the handout on swimming safety I gave you last week. Because today we're going to discuss what to do if your swim buddy gets in trouble. I'm going to need two volunteers."

MacKenzie and I immediately gave each other the evil eye! Just the mere thought of us working together as partners was beyond repulsive.

I think our teacher must have seen our reactions and decided that making us wear the school's smelly, saggy, scratchy regulation swimsuits was NOT enough torture.

"Let's see. How about . . . MISS MAXWELL . . . and MISS HOLLISTER?"

OUR GYM TEACHER, FORCING
MACKENZIE AND ME TO BE
SWIMMING PARTNERS

MacKenzie and I both rolled our eyes and groaned.

I immediately started feeling a little nauseous and I hadn't even swallowed any of the nasty, germy pool water yet.

"Okay! Let's do some role-playing. Miss Hollister, you'll be the swim buddy on the shore. And Miss Maxwell, you'll be the swim buddy struggling in the water."

Well, one thing was for sure. I wouldn't have to do a lot of acting to be totally convincing in THAT role.

"Actually, I was w-wondering if you maybe could pick someone else?" I stammered nervously. "I'm really not that good of a swim—"

"Come on, Miss Maxwell, hustle! In the pool! NOW!" she yelled at me like I was there trying out for the Olympic swimming team or something.

So I took a running leap, grabbed my nose, and did a cannonball into the pool. . .

SPLASH!

OMG! I hit the water like a brick. It literally knocked the wind out of me. I coughed and wheezed as I paddled for my life.

"Okay, Miss Hollister, imagine you're at the beach and you notice your swim buddy struggling in the water. What do—"

"Wait," MacKenzie interrupted. "Which beach is it?"

"I don't know . . . ANY beach!" the gym teacher snapped impatiently. "That doesn't matter."

"I know! How about . . . the HAMPTONS?!" MacKenzie said excitedly.

"Fine! A beach at the Hamptons! And you're worried your swim buddy might be in trouble. What would you do?"

"What would I do? Wow! That's a hard one. Well, for starters, I probably WOULDN'T go to the Hamptons! We vacationed there last year, and there were WAY too many tourists," she answered smugly. "Hey! Put ME on a Brazilian beach! With an air-conditioned cabana, raspberry-melon iced tea, and lots of cute surfer boys!"

"You're completely missing the point! This is about water safety!" the gym teacher said, flustered.

How DENSE could that girl be?

"Hurry up and answer the stinkin' question, MacKenzie!" I yelled. "I can't paddle much longer!"

MacKenzie scratched her head and gave the gym teacher a long, blank stare.

"Um, is this, like, a multiple-choice question or something?" she asked, twirling her hair. "I've heard the beaches in Hawaii are to die for!"

"Getting! Stomach! Cramps!" I panted. "HEEELP!!"

"Hollister, you're supposed to be aware of your swim buddy at all times!" the gym teacher yelled. "YOUR swim buddy is possibly in TROUBLE! Now go jump in the water and save her!"

"Who? ME?! I DON'T think so!" MacKenzie replied coolly. "I just curled my hair this morning."

"WORST! (glug) . . . SWIM BUDDY! (glug) . . . EVER!!!" I gurgled, choking on more water.

Then my head went under. I can't remember what

happened after that. I guess I blacked out and my teacher jumped in to rescue me. That's what I was told, anyway. However, what I DO remember is waking up on the tile floor next to the pool.

I was surrounded by a bunch of snickering classmates, a not-so-happy gym teacher and my BFFs.

↑
ME

That's when I felt something weird around my waist.

And when I looked down, I discovered I was wearing a yellow doughnut-shaped inner-tube thingy with baby ducks on it.

It wasn't NEARLY as cute as the sea horse my teacher had flat-out refused to let me wear in the pool just last week.

Go figure!

"You're keeping that thing on for the rest of the class today. Got it, Maxwell?" my gym teacher said drily. "If you're having that much trouble swimming in one metre of water, you're going to need all the help you can get."

"Wait a minute!" I exclaimed. "Are you saying I almost drowned in only ONE metre of water?!! That's barely up to my shoulders! I thought for sure I was in the deep end!"

My teacher sighed and shook her head.

OOPS! My BAD ☹!!

Then she launched into another one of her stern lectures.

"Listen up, people! Water safety is serious business! The buddy system is NO joke! Lives are at stake! To ensure that everyone completely understands these concepts, tomorrow I'll be giving you a written test! Sorry! But after what just happened here today, I really don't have a choice," she said, and glared at MacKenzie.

Every kid in the class groaned this time, including me.

Our teacher continued. "Please read over the handout I gave you. You really need to learn this stuff. Any questions?"

I could tell the entire class was pretty ticked off, based on the dirty looks MacKenzie was getting.

"Hey, don't blame ME!" MacKenzie shrugged and batted her eyes all innocent-like.

Then she whipped around and pointed her finger right in my face . . .

It's all HER fault! Blame the
DORK IN THE DOUGHNUT!

I could NOT believe that girl just threw me under the bus like that.

AND I definitely didn't appreciate her little "dork in the doughnut" comment!

If MacKenzie hadn't sat there very STUPIDLY planning her next beach vacation while watching me DROWN, we wouldn't be having a written test.

In GYM, of all classes.

It was all HER fault!

But of course MacKenzie is Miss PERFECT!

And all of the CCPs were rolling their eyes and whispering about ME!

The "DORK in the doughnut"!

UGH! I give up!

Next time . . .

Just let me DROWN!

☹!!

AAAAAAAAAAAAAAAHHH!

(That was me screaming!)

I was totally FREAKED out by what I saw in the halls when I got to school this morning.

It was surreal! I felt like I'd walked into one of my worst nightmares. I wanted to just call my parents and go home.

WHO did this to me?!!! And WHY?!!!

Only three other people at school knew about it.

"It" being that horribly embarrassing photo that my bratty sister, Brianna, accidentally texted to the ENTIRE world.

Okay! Well, maybe NOT the entire world.

Just CHLOE, ZOEY and BRANDON!

Just looking at that photo gives me a migraine...

Chloe and Zoey were really upset and have pinkie sworn to me THREE times that they had NOTHING to do with it. And I really want to believe them.

So that leaves... BRANDON. But WHY would he do this? Or give my picture to someone who would?

Anyway, this is what I saw when I arrived at school this morning...

"VOTE NIKKI MAXWELL FOR SWEETHEART PRINCESS!" POSTERS WERE EVERYWHERE!

But the most humiliating thing is that everyone thinks I plastered those hideous posters around the school because I WANT to be voted Sweetheart Princess.

When in reality, I DIDN'T put up the posters! And I DON'T want to be voted Sweetheart Princess! Okay, so maybe I wouldn't mind all that much if it actually happened.

But come on! I'm the biggest loser in the entire school. Like, WHO would even vote for me?!

And even if there WAS the possibility of getting a few random votes from students, I'm sure my very creepy picture made them change their minds.

This little STUNT had MacKenzie Hollister written ALL over it! I would give anything to know how MacKenzie got her grubby little hands on my photo.

Thank goodness my BFFs were there to help me rip the posters down.

It took us, like, FOREVER!

ME, CHLOE AND ZOEY TEARING
DOWN THOSE HIDEOUS POSTERS

Why in the world would MacKenzie do this when she knows I'm not going to the dance? Maybe she's just trying to rub it in my face that I don't have a date. I'm so sick of her little mind games!

Then, to make matters worse, I got a text from Brandon during lunch.

* * * * *

FROM BRANDON:
You looked kind of freaky in that picture.
But you're STILL my friend :-p!
12:36 p.m.

* * * * *

It's going to take me YEARS of intense therapy to get over all of the traumatic experiences I've had in middle school just this past week!

AAAAAAAAAAAAHHHHH!!

(That was me screaming AGAIN!)

Today in swimming class we had a skills test on diving.

"Now, class, the object of this skills test is to measure your ability to dive AND retrieve the objects from the bottom of the pool as quickly as possible," our teacher explained. "You'll be diving for seven plastic rings."

Come on! What's the point? What are we training for? A dolphin show or something?! Why doesn't the teacher just sell tickets to see us perform and throw us fish as a reward when we do a good job? I'm just sayin'!

But get this! I couldn't believe there was no ambulance or some elite emergency team here to rescue us.

You know, like the ones you always see on the sidelines at our football games.

Didn't it dawn on our teacher that we might need CPR or maybe even oxygen?

Or how about one of those supersized rescue-hook thingies to pull us out of the water in the event of an emergency?

MacKenzie was next in line to take her skills test. When the teacher yelled "DIVE!" MacKenzie dove into the pool, barely making a splash. Within seconds she had scooped up all of the rings and was back out of the pool with the fastest time in the entire class.

She waved and blew kisses to everyone like she had just won a gold medal in the Olympics or something.

That girl is so VAIN!

However, I was not the least bit intimidated.

Dad had purchased everything I needed for my skills test from a yard sale last summer. . .

ME, READY TO DIVE IN MY SCUBA GEAR

Anyway, when my teacher hollered "DIVE!" I jumped
in and grabbed all the rings in record time. Even
faster than MacKenzie!

My gym teacher congratulated me on my remarkable performance. But then she got an attitude about the whole thing and gave me a . . .

big fat D ☹!

I was so DISGUSTED!

"Sorry, Miss Maxwell," my teacher said. "But you're diving for plastic rings, NOT sunken treasure! No scuba gear is allowed!!"

Apparently, it was against the pool rules. But HOW was I supposed to know THAT?!

The only sign about rules I saw said . . .

WCD POOL RULES
1. NO running!
2. NO eating!
3. NO horseplay!
4. NO peeing in the pool!
5. NO floating toys!

There was nothing on that list that said . . .

NO SCUBA GEAR!

That's when I totally lost it and yelled at my teacher. "Sorry, lady, but I'm NOT some humpback whale capable of diving to the deepest, darkest, most dangerous depths of the pool. I NEED my mask, wet suit, regulator, tank and scuba fins. Besides, the water is so deep my eyeballs could pop out. And I could die from decompression sickness.

"Worse yet, YOU didn't even bother to have an ambulance here just in case I needed to be rushed to the hospital! So let me see YOU dive to the bottom of the pool without having a massive stroke or something!"

But I just said that in my head, so no one else heard it but me.

That diving skills test was SO unfair! I should definitely get a do-over!! I'm just sayin'!! ☹!!

I'm really starting to worry about my grade in swimming. If I get lower than a C as a final grade, my teacher will request a meeting with my parents.

OMG! What if I end up losing my bug extermination scholarship and can't attend this school any longer?

And as if I don't already have enough problems, I noticed Brandon staring at me in the halls today. He actually tried to talk to me in bio, but I totally ignored him.

AGAIN!

But then things got even weirder!

I was working in the library and minding my own business, and guess who just popped in like he owned the place or something??!!

BRANDON ☹!!

I know! I couldn't believe it either!

Anyway, he asked if he could talk to me, and I said yes, but right then I was really busy putting away books.

Then he said, "Well, I'll help you put them away, and then we can talk while we're working."

And I said, "Actually, you CAN'T help me because you don't know where the books are supposed to go on the shelves."

That's when he suggested that HE could help by handing ME the books so I could place them on the shelves.

He was being very nice, sweet and helpful, and getting on my LAST nerve all at the same time!

So he was handing me books, and I was putting them on the shelves.

Which made me SUPERnervous because he kept kind of . . . staring at me.

BRANDON KIND OF STARES AT ME WHILE
WE'RE PUTTING AWAY LIBRARY BOOKS.

Finally he cleared his throat. "Nikki, I just wanted to let you know that I felt really bad about you getting in trouble in bio for trying to do something nice for me."

"Like I said before, it wasn't that big of a deal!"

"Well, it was to ME. So I want to do something nice for you."

"Actually, that's not necessary. It was just a stupid card!"

"I don't think it was stupid."

"Well, I do!" I shot back.

Brandon stared at the floor. "Anyway, I thought maybe we could hang out at Crazy Burger this Saturday. I know the last time I mentioned it, you said you didn't want to go because you were SUPERbusy!"

I could not believe he actually said that to me!

Not the part about hanging out at Crazy Burger. But that part about me NOT wanting to go to Crazy Burger because I was SUPERbusy.

"WHAAAT?! No way! Brandon, YOU said you couldn't go to Crazy Burger because YOU were SUPERbusy!"

"HUH?! No, Nikki! YOU told ME you were too busy and couldn't go. It was at your locker. I wanted to go, but that Saturday and Sunday didn't work out."

"Actually, you kind of stood me up," I said.

"No, I didn't. When I tried to explain what happened, you shut me down."

"That's NOT what happened. I was trying to talk to YOU and you just walked away!"

Lately, whenever we tried to have a conversation, we ended up fighting. Brandon and I just stared at each other in frustration. . .

For some strange reason, we were having major communication problems.

I knew in my gut that something was wrong! But I didn't have the slightest idea what it was or how to fix it.

Finally Brandon sighed and brushed his hair out of his eyes.

"Okay. So, how about Crazy Burger on Saturday? At six thirty p.m. If you're not too busy," he said, giving me a crooked smile.

"Okay, sure! If YOU'RE not too busy!" I said, smiling back at him.

Then we both kind of stared at each other and blushed.

All of this smiling, staring and blushing went on, like, FOREVER!

So, it was official. Brandon and I were hanging out at Crazy Burger on Saturday.

I couldn't wait to tell Chloe and Zoey the exciting news.

But I didn't have to. . .

Chloe and Zoey were secretly spying on us the entire time?!

I could NOT believe my BFFs would stoop so low as to do something like that to Brandon and me!

Especially during a very private and personal conversation about our friendship.

Chloe and Zoey are always sticking their big fat noses in my personal business. But it's mostly because the two of them really care about me.

I have to admit . . .

They're the best friends EVER!!

☺!!

I'm still so excited about Crazy Burger that I barely got any sleep last night.

Of course I couldn't wait to see Brandon in bio.

SQUEEE ☺!

We blushed, smiled and made goo-goo eyes the ENTIRE hour. I could see MacKenzie and Jessica staring at us and whispering like crazy. But I didn't care.

To be honest, I don't remember a single word my teacher said about today's lesson. But it was the BEST. CLASS. EVER!

I'm SO happy Brandon and I are FINALLY getting along again. I just hope spending time together at Crazy Burger will help strengthen our friendship.

But right now my immediate problem is that I don't have the slightest idea what to wear on our first date.

I don't want my outfit to be too dressy, but not too casual, either. It needs to be . . . PERFECT!

I just stood there staring inside my closet for what seemed like FOREVER! But unfortunately, I didn't see anything that was PERFECT ☹!

ME, LOOKING FOR THE PERFECT OUTFIT!

I was DESPERATE! So I decided to take DRASTIC action.

I knew it would be dangerous because of the risk of exhaustion. But I didn't really have a choice.

I was going to TRY ON all of my clothes superfast and mix and match tops and bottoms until I came up with a SUPERCUTE outfit! Also known as a . . . TRY-ON-A-THON!

When the smoke finally cleared, my TRY-ON-A-THON was a HUGE success!

I came up with the most FAB OUTFIT ever . . . !

ME, MODELING MY FAB OUTFIT!

Now all I have to do is get through the meal
WITHOUT:

1. dropping my hamburger in my lap.

2. accidentally squirting ketchup on Brandon.

3. laughing so hard that soda dribbles out of my nose.

MUST.

NOT.

FREAK.

OUT!

☺!!

OMG! Today's the big day! Brandon and I have a date at Crazy Burger in just a few hours!!

SQUEEE ☺!

By the time I showered, did my hair, and got dressed, it was 6:15 p.m. and time for my mom to drive me to the restaurant.

I was a nervous wreck!

I had sat next to Brandon in bio, like, forever. But the thought of sitting next to him at Crazy Burger was more scary than those *Friday the 13th* movies that my parents refused to let me watch.

"Hi, Nikki!" he said, smiling. "It's cool that we're FINALLY getting to hang out here."

I quickly checked behind me just to make sure he wasn't talking to someone else named Nikki.

"Hi, Brandon!" I said, blushing profusely.

For the next five minutes, we just sat there nervously sipping our sodas and staring at each other with these big, dorky grins plastered across our faces. It was SO romantic! Well, kind of.

It felt like the butterflies in my stomach were having a big party. And some of them must have flown up to my brain, because I could barely think straight.

Brandon seemed more quiet than usual too.

Then I picked up the paper thingy from my straw and started wrapping it around and around my finger while I tried to think of something funny, witty, or interesting to say. I came up with . . .

"Hmm, I wonder what stuff is in that ketchup?"

That's when Brandon picked up the ketchup bottle and started reading off all of the ingredients. "Well, it says tomato concentrate, distilled vinegar, corn syrup, salt, spice, onion powder and other ingredients."

I grabbed a piece of the straw paper thingy and made a giant spit wad and shot it right out of my straw, and it landed on the table in front of Brandon's glass. *SMACK!*

Brandon was surprised that I knew how to make spit wads.

Then he took a few sips of his soda.

But when his straw made those loud slurpy noises, like *SKURR—SKURR*, he coughed nervously and almost knocked over his glass.

Then we stared at each other some more. Next I took the salt shaker and poured salt into my hand and made these little miniature mountains while Brandon watched.

Suddenly his stomach started making these loud grumbling sounds, probably because he was hungry or something.

"OMG! Brandon, your stomach sounds just like a jet engine!" I teased. You should have seen the look on his face. I thought he was going to DIE of embarrassment!

Then, finally, our burgers came . . . !

OMG! They were crazy delicious! Soon our nervous jitters went away and we actually had an intelligent conversation.

He gave me an update on Fuzzy Friends, his work for the school newspaper and his photography projects.

I told him about losing a hair chunk at Salon Brianna, Mrs Wallabanger's grandson and the horrors of swimming class.

We both laughed until our sides hurt. It was amazing how Brandon was just so . . .

FUNNY and NICE!

Then things got SUPERserious. He said he felt awful when he heard that someone had plastered those crazy posters of me around the school. He said he's ALLERGIC to mean people!

We both agreed that MacKenzie was probably behind it.

I really wanted to ask him if he had any idea how she'd got her hands on that photo since Brianna had only emailed it to Chloe, Zoey and him.

But I was sure he would have been highly insulted and disappointed that I'd accuse him of helping MacKenzie pull a nasty prank like that. So I decided NOT to mention it right then.

Somehow, we ended up talking about the Sweetheart Dance.

"So, are you going?" I asked.

"No. But I would if the right person asked me."

"Does that mean the wrong person asked you?"

"Yeah, MacKenzie actually came to my birthday party and asked me. But I told her no. Since then she's been hanging around, trying to get me to change my mind. She even offered to have her dad make a sizable donation to Fuzzy Friends if I'd go with her. Hey, we need the money badly, but . . ." His voice trailed off.

I started playing with the straw paper thingy again as my mind raced.

So MacKenzie had asked Brandon to the dance?!

And he turned her down?!

I was SUPERhappy AND relieved to hear that news.

Now I could ask him to the dance!

If I could just muster up the courage.

"Well, maybe someone else wants to ask you but she's afraid you might say no," I said, blushing.

"Really?!" Brandon blinked in surprise. "Actually, I'd probably . . . no, definitely say YES! Like, IF she actually asked," he said, staring at me.

That was my cue!

Brandon was basically asking ME to ask HIM to the dance!

"Well . . . um, about the dance. I wanted to ask you . . . if you . . . um, think, er . . . WE . . . will have another

BLIZZARD?! We got a whopping twenty centimetres of snow last time!" I babbled like an idiot.

STRIKE ONE!

Brandon continued to stare at me. "Nope. Do you want to ask me anything else?"

"Actually, there IS something I'd like to ask."

"Okay . . ."

"So, would you . . . like to, um, have DESSERT??!! I hear the red velvet chocolate cake at this place is to DIE for!"

Brandon smiled and nodded his head. "Sure, Nikki! That sounds great!"

I wanted to kick myself. STRIKE TWO!!

"Um, Brandon, there's j—just one last thing I want to ask you . . ." I stammered nervously.

"Wait. Let me guess!" Brandon teased. "You want to know if . . . I want ice cream?"

"No! Not that!" I replied.

"Hot fudge on the side, with whipped cream?"

"NO!" I giggled.

"I know! Those little sprinkle thingies!"

"NOOO!" I shouted.

"Then, WHAT . . . ?!" Brandon asked in mock frustration.

"I want to know if you'd . . . you know . . . go to the Sweetheart Dance with me!" I blurted out, blushing profusely.

Suddenly Brandon got this SUPERserious look on his face and started fidgeting with his straw. Okay, now I was really nervous. Maybe asking him was a big mistake.

"Actually, Nikki, there's just no way I could—"

"That's fine! Really!" I interrupted. "I totally understand. I asked you at the last minute and everything!"

I gave him a weak smile. But deep down inside I felt so hurt I wanted to burst into tears.

"Actually, Nikki, there's just no way I could say NO to you!" Brandon said as he brushed his hair out of his eyes and gave me that crooked smile.

That's when I blushed again and smiled at him.

And then he blushed and smiled at me. All of this blushing and smiling went on, like, FOREVER!

So not only did I have a really great time at Crazy Burger, but now . . .

I'M GOING TO THE SWEETHEART DANCE WITH BRANDON!!

SQUEEE ☺!!

I am SOOO excited!

ME, DOING MY SNOOPY "HAPPY DANCE"!!

I can't wait to call Chloe and Zoey and tell them the FANTASTIC news!

Although, there's a slight chance my BFFs already know, if they were at Crazy Burger hiding under our table SPYING on us. AGAIN!

I guess we'll be able to go on a TRIPLE DATE together after all. Just like we'd planned!

SQUEEE!!! ☺!!

OMG! This is going to be SOOO romantic!!

ME, HOLDING MY HEART AND
SWOONING MASSIVELY!!

It's hard to believe that I'm actually going to the Sweetheart Dance with Brandon.

SQUEEE ☺!!

I think Chloe and Zoey are even more excited about it than I am. They've already called me a dozen times and I just told them the news an hour ago.

The dress code is formal attire, which means girls get to wear floor-length dresses! You know, like Cinderella and all of the Disney Princesses.

How COOL is THAT?!

Chloe and Zoey already have their dresses.

But being the great friends that they are, they agreed to meet at the mall to help find the perfect one for ME.

Anyway, I must have tried on fifty dresses...

But they were either too FRUMPY . . .

Or too FRILLY!

Or too FORMAL . . .

Or too FUNKY!

We came back from the mall empty-handed.

Of course I was pretty bummed out.

It didn't help matters that we ran into Jessica, and she saw me shopping for a dress. And since she's MacKenzie's BFF, that means she's going to BLAB all of my personal business.

But the good news is that there are STILL four more shopping days until the dance!

I'm pretty SURE I'll find the perfect dress.

Somewhere!

I mean, how HARD could it be?!

☺!!

Okay, I'm starting to PANIC! Mom said she would take me shopping for a dress on Wednesday. But that's only two days before the dance!! She said if we can't find a new dress, I can just use the ~~very ugly~~ silver and seaweed-green bridesmaid dress from my aunt Kim's wedding.

Mom, are you KA-RAY-ZEE?! I REFUSE to go to the Sweetheart Dance looking like some kind of MUTANT FISH!

Sorry, Mom, but this is a formal dance — NOT a COSTUME party!

Anyway, after dinner I got the sweetest text from Brandon.

SQUEEE!! I think hanging out at Crazy Burger really helped our friendship.

* * * * *

FROM BRANDON:

Hi Nikki,

Looking forward 2 going 2 the dance with U. Good luck finding a dress that will actually make U look beautiful!

7:39 p.m.

* * * * *

Wait a minute!! Did he just say . . . ?!

Now I REALLY need to BURN this DRESS!

☹!

Today in gym class we were having timed swimming races against each other.

For some strange reason, whenever I try to swim more than six metres, my legs cramp up and get stuck in really weird positions. I look kind of like one of Brianna's old Barbie dolls with TWO broken legs. And once my legs are all messed up, I start to panic and rarely make it to the other end of the pool.

But mostly I was SUPERworried because this race was going to be 50% of our swimming grade ☹!

Our gym teacher blew her whistle. *TWEET, TWEET!!* "Next group, please take the starting line!"

It was finally time for MY race to begin.

Chloe gave me a big hug and jazz hands for good luck. Zoey gave me a hug too and recited another of her inspirational quotes, this time from John Lennon . . .

"'When you're drowning, you don't say "I would be incredibly pleased if someone would have the foresight to notice me drowning and come and help me," you just scream!'"

I was like, "Thanks a million for that, Zoey!"

I think that quote was supposed to encourage me. But quite frankly, it scared the SNOT out of me! You just SCREAM?!! What kind of advice is THAT?!

Oh! And did I forget to mention that I was swimming against MacKenzie and three CCPs?

"So, Nikki! I see you're going to attempt to swim today without your scuba suit or ridiculous floaty toys." MacKenzie sneered.

Her friends snickered. I just rolled my eyes at that girl. I wanted to say something. But right then my knees were so shaky I was more worried about accidentally falling face-first into the water before the race even got started.

Our teacher stood on a podium to begin the race.
"Swimmers, take your mark. Get set . . ." *TWEET!*

ME, TRYING NOT TO FALL FACE-FIRST
INTO THE WATER

I dove into the water and began swimming frantically.

Although we had just got started, I could already clearly see I was way behind.

Yep! Dead last! It was so HUMILIATING ☹!

To make matters worse, I was slowing down and my leg muscles were starting to cramp up.

Finally I stopped swimming and started to doggy-paddle.

MacKenzie was in the lead, and the three other girls were close behind her. I wanted to give up!

That's when I looked over my right shoulder and caught a glimpse of a dark shadow slightly behind me. Actually, it looked a lot like a . . . shark's fin?!

I took another look and . . . YES! It WAS a shark's fin, just several metres away. I couldn't believe my eyes!

OMG! I think I actually peed in the pool!

And judging from the size of its fin, that thing was GIGANTIC! Out of sheer terror, I started swimming as fast as I could.

OMG! WHAT IS **THAT**?!

A shark in the pool?! How in the HECK did that get in here? I wondered as I swam for my life. I came up with three possible theories.

It could have been living in the Westchester County sewers like those alligators, pythons and other scary creatures we hear about in the news.

Or if it was in the drainage system, it probably got too big for the pipes and burst through the drain and into the pool.

Or maybe it escaped from the Westchester Zoo and was swimming down the creek behind our school when it decided to stop off at the pool for a quick LUNCH!

One thing was for sure. I had no intention of becoming its next MEAL.

You know, yummy Nikki Nuggets dipped in chlorine.

I must have had a surge of adrenaline or something because I kept swimming faster and faster until I reached the end of the pool.

Then I jumped out and zipped right past my teacher, screaming at the top of my lungs . . .

SHARK! SHARK!
RUN FOR YOUR LIFE!

MACKENZIE, TRYING TO FIGURE OUT
HOW I BEAT HER TO THE FINISH LINE

Hey, there was no way I was going to hang around
poolside. Sharks swim ashore, attack their prey and
then drag them back into the deep to be eaten!

At least, that's what they do in movies and on TV! And personally, I wasn't taking any chances. So I kept running until I got to the very top of the bleachers. Only then did I check behind me to make sure that shark hadn't followed me up there. Hey, it could happen!

That's when I heard my gym teacher make an announcement over the loudspeaker. "May I have your attention, please? I'd like to congratulate Nikki Maxwell. She not only won first place in the swimming race, but she set a new school record for the fifty-metre swim. That's an A+ for you, Miss Maxwell. Job well done! Please come and pick up your award certificate."

I cautiously walked back down to the pool, where Chloe and Zoey gave me a big hug.

"Did you not see that humungous shark in the water?" I gasped.

"All we saw was you give MacKenzie a good beatdown in that race!" Zoey gushed.

"OMG! You won by a mile!" Chloe giggled. "You were out of the pool before she even finished."

"But I could have sworn I saw a SHARK!"

My BFFs walked to the other end of the pool and returned with something big and shiny with a huge fin. Only, it DIDN'T have pointy teeth.

"THIS is NOT a SHARK, Nikki!" Chloe said.

"Um . . . try plastic SCUBA FIN!" Zoey giggled.

"Sorry, guys! But it looked like a shark to ME!" I muttered.

OMG! I was SO embarrassed.

Anyway, after winning the race and then getting fifty extra-credit points for breaking the school record, I ended up earning an A as the final grade in my swimming class!

That stupid class had been kicking my butt all month. I never would have thunk this could happen.

Woo-hoo! I was beyond HAPPY!

And now the coach actually wants me to join the girls' swimming team.

How CRAZY is THAT??!!

☺!!

Today after school, Mom and I went shopping to try and finally find a dress for the Sweetheart Dance. First we went to the dress section of Forever Sixteen, but the clothing racks were empty and there wasn't a single dress in sight.

A pile of broken clothes hangers littered the floor. It looked just like the aftermath of an elephant stampede!

Then we went to five more stores, and all of them were in the same condition.

"No place in this ENTIRE mall has a dress?" Mom asked, clearly frustrated. "I can't believe that! Let's try finding a sales clerk."

We were at a fancy department store, and we finally found a sales clerk hiding behind the checkout counter. In the fetal position!

"Excuse me, ma'am," Mom said to her. "We're looking for a dress. Could you help us, please?"

"D-d-dress?!" the sales clerk gasped in horror. "Did you just say . . . DRESS?! AAAAHHH!!!" she screamed hysterically and dashed out of the emergency exit door.

What I didn't realise was that thousands of

desperate middle school and high school girls had
descended upon the mall and turned dress ~~shopping~~
hunting into a brutal gladiator sport. . .

Back home, Mom suggested again that I wear that "adorable" ~~mermaid~~ bridesmaid dress.

EWW!!

Clearly, she has a bad memory, because that thing is HIDEOUS!

Sorry, Mom, but vomit green is NOT my colour.

And that dress is impossible to walk in! It's so tight around my legs that it looks like a giant fish tail.

While the other bridesmaids walked gracefully to the "Wedding March" song, I flopped my way down the aisle like a human-sized catfish or something!

Those rug burns were pure agony!

It was getting late and I was running out of time!

The last thing I wanted to do was to traumatise

Brandon by showing up at the dance looking like a MUTANT FISH GIRL or something.

Right now I'm SO frustrated that I'm seriously considering just NOT going to the dance.

Why is my life so hopelessly

CRUDDY?!

☹!!!

I had an unexpected visitor after school today! I was in my room doing my French homework when suddenly I was rudely interrupted . . .

"There you are, Miss Nikki! I, Miss Bri-Bri, Fashionista and STYLIST to the Stars, have been looking all over for YOU!" Brianna exclaimed. "Come quickly, dah-ling! Miss Bri-Bri must style you before her next appointment!"

"Don't take another step toward me, or you'll be sorry!" I screamed. "I have a French book in my hand, and I'm NOT afraid to use it. Last time you TOTALLY ruined my hair! Are you even a licenced professional?"

"But all of that was my assistant's fault. I fired Hans. Now come! Miss Bri-Bri shall make you booty-ful! Yes?"

"NO WAY! Miss Bri-Bri can go jump in le LAKE! I'm still mad at you!"

"Zen I shall make it up to you. Miss Bri-Bri pinkie promises! Or she'll eat a thousand boogers!"

WHAT kind of promise was that?! I was pretty sure Miss Bri-Bri ate boogers anyway! On the other hand, whatever dress she had to offer me couldn't be any uglier than the one I already had.

I didn't have much to lose! Well, other than another hair chunk. But that was a risk I was willing to take for the dance. And for Brandon!

"Okay, Brianna! I'm going to give you ONE more chance! So don't screw this up!" I warned.

"Dah-ling! We have much work to do! Please follow my new assistant, Miss Penelope."

Miss Penelope waved at me and then grabbed my arm and led me down the hall.

She was wearing lots of rings and bracelets, glittery nail polish, hot-pink lip gloss and drawn-on cat-eye glasses that matched Brianna's.

"Dah-ling! Here we are! Welcome to BOUTIQUE BRIANNA!" Miss Bri-Bri announced, taking me into the upstairs bathroom. "Miss Bri-Bri has designed a gazillion booty-ful dresses for very famous and important people, like Princess Sugar Plum, Selena Gomez, Beyoncé, and Mrs Claus! And I have created zee perfect dress for you, dah-ling! Miss Penelope, please show Miss Nikki to zee dressing room," she ordered.

Suddenly Brianna raised her hand to her ear, whispered something to Miss Penelope, and then frowned.

"What was zat, Miss Penelope?" she asked. "You are on zee phone with Dora zee Explorer and Boots zee Monkey? You say Boots needs new boots? Very well, dah-ling! Pencil him in before my six o'clock appointment with SpongeBob!"

Brianna turned to me and smiled apologetically. "Please excuse zee interruption, dah-ling. Miss Penelope's up to her knuckles in phone calls and paperwork. Now, where were we? Oh yes! Zee dress for YOU!"

She walked up to the bathtub and pulled back the shower curtain. *SWISH* . . . *!!*

"NOW, MISS NIKKI, PLEASE STEP
INTO YOUR DRESSING ROOM!"

I was really shocked to see a clothing bag with my name on it hanging inside the "dressing room".

But I was afraid it might be a trick.

"Hmm . . . You want me to step inside?" I eyed her suspiciously. "Why? Is this a prank? Did you put a shark in there or something?!"

"Of course not! My boutique has a no-shark policy, dah-ling!" Brianna replied, slightly offended.

"All right, already!" I muttered under my breath as I climbed into the tub.

Brianna closed the curtain behind me. *SWISH!*

"I'll check back with you in a few minutes, dah-ling. As soon as I finish up with Sasha and Malia Obama."

Although the clothing bag looked new, I expected to find Brianna's ratty old hot-pink Barbie robe inside.

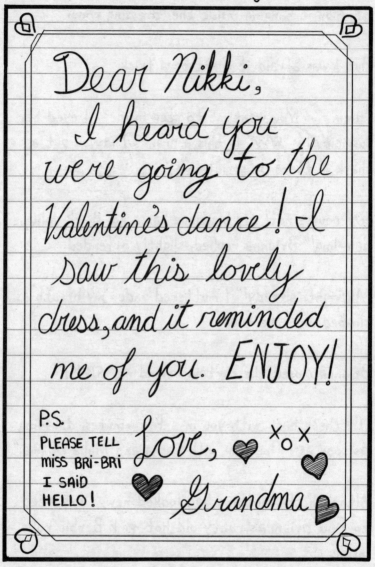

Dear Nikki,

I heard you were going to the Valentine's dance! I saw this lovely dress, and it reminded me of you. ENJOY!

P.S.
PLEASE TELL
MISS BRI-BRI
I SAID
HELLO!

Love, ♥ ˣoˣ ♥

♥ Grandma ♥

I was right! Brianna WAS up to something!

That delusional little SNEAK had contacted
Grandma and arranged a wonderful surprise . . .
The most BEAUTIFUL dress EVER!!

It was absolutely PERFECT for the dance. I couldn't
wait to show my BFFs.

SQUEEEEEE!!!

All of the CCP girls will be so JEALOUS!

I paid Miss Bri-Bri for her "services" with a bag of Skittles.

"See, dah-ling?! Miss Bri-Bri made you a very BOOTY-FUL dress! Yes?!"

"Miss Bri-Bri TOTALLY ROCKED!" I giggled.

"Then we can forget zee little haircut problem?!"

"Forgotten!" I said, and gave ~~Brianna~~ Miss Bri-Bri a big hug.

Then I excitedly rushed off to my room to try on my new dress.

☺!!

Today the entire school was buzzing about the dance. Students excitedly lined up between classes to vote for Sweetheart Princess. The latest gossip was that MacKenzie was going to win by a landslide.

I avoided voting entirely. It was just a reminder of MacKenzie's nasty prank, which I was trying very hard to forget.

I still didn't have the slightest idea how she got her hands on that Salon Brianna photo. Maybe it was my imagination, but in every class it seemed like kids were staring at me and whispering ☹!

So I just zoned out and spent the entire day staring at the clock and counting down the hours until the Sweetheart Dance ☺! 10, 9, 8, 7, 6, 5, 4 . . . !

Before I knew it, school was over and the dance was starting in less than an hour. I took one last look at myself in the mirror.

On the inside, I felt SUPERinsecure. But on the outside, I looked like a real princess. . .

Well, MINUS the scrawny arms and shoulders ☹!

Mom's new *Get Toned in 20 Minutes DVD* was a total rip-off. I had used it for forty minutes after school to tone up my arms, but they STILL looked EXACTLY the same. What's up with THAT? Mom definitely needs to get her money back!

For some reason, I was having a severe case of the last-minute jitters. I felt super self-conscious about EVERYTHING.

I sighed and popped a Tic Tac into my mouth. Then I stuffed my phone into my purse, grabbed my coat and headed downstairs.

Suddenly my phone chimed. I was pretty sure it was a text from Chloe and Zoey letting me know they were on their way to pick me up.

There was just NO WAY I was going to risk public humiliation by riding in my dad's ROACH MOBILE! It was MY brilliant idea to have Zoey's mom drive us there and Chloe's mom drive us home!

But surprisingly, the text wasn't from Chloe or Zoey.

It was from BRANDON! SQUEEEEEE ☺!!

I guessed that he was probably sending me a message telling me he couldn't wait to see me or something. You know, like in all of those romance novels. SQUEEEEEE ☺!!

Swooning massively, I held my breath and read his pre-Sweetheart-Dance text message out loud:

@BRANDON

BAD NEWS! JUST CAUGHT THE FLU. CAN'T GO TO THE DANCE.

SORRY☹!!

I blinked in disbelief and read it again. This had to be some kind of mistake!

Obviously, some other dude named Brandon had just decided, at the very last minute, to "TEXT DUMP" his poor unsuspecting date!!

And then sent it to ME by accident!

NOT ☹!!

I felt like I had been hit in the stomach. By a bowling ball.

WHY would Brandon do this to me?!!!

Okay. Maybe because he was SICK! But STILL! What harm is a little flu bug between really good friends?!!

Since the dance was such a big deal, I was hoping he would have gallantly ignored his fever and nausea and just showed up with a barf bag or something.

If I had the flu, I would have done that for HIM!

Hey! If I had been hit by a bus, I would have come to the dance in a full-body cast with some SUPERcute matching earrings!

This was the last straw!

I felt like I was on a crazy emotional roller coaster, plummeting into a deep, dark bottomless pit. And I wanted off!

I knew I couldn't blame Brandon for getting sick! But why did he wait until the very last minute?!

And why did he drop the bomb on me in a very tacky text message instead of apologising profusely in person? Or at least in a phone call?!

It was like he wasn't thinking about my feelings at all!

Deep down in my gut, I suspected that Brandon was not sick at all. He had probably taken

MacKenzie up on her Fuzzy Friends cash offer.

And after changing his mind about going to the dance with me, he wasn't brave enough to tell me to my face.

I was stupid and delusional to think we'd ever become good friends. I really hated to admit it, but MacKenzie was right ☹!

I dragged myself back to my room, slammed my door shut and collapsed on my bed.

Then I sobbed hysterically into my pillow.

OMG! I felt beyond HORRIBLE. My heart was actually hurting.

I had been lying there for what seemed, like, FOREVER, when suddenly I heard footsteps and two familiar voices outside my door.

I closed my eyes and groaned. Oh, CRUD! I'd forgotten to call Chloe and Zoey . . . !

They burst into my room like a hurricane.

"Nikki! Your favorite BFFs are here!" Zoey squealed happily. "Are you ready?"

"Don't be TARDY for the PARTY!" Chloe shouted, and gave me jazz hands.

I slowly sat up on the edge of my bed, sniffed and dabbed at my tears.

My BFFs immediately froze and stared at me in shock with their mouths hanging open.

"OMG! Nikki! What's wrong?!" they both shrieked.

"I'm n—not going to the d—dance!" I muttered. "Brandon just texted me. He says he's . . . SICK!"

"WHAT?!" they gasped.

That's when I totally lost it and burst into

TEARS. . .

I FEEL AWFUL! I CAN'T BELIEVE BRANDON
JUST STOOD ME UP LIKE THIS!!

I had a complete and massive meltdown. Chloe and
Zoey both hugged me. They were about to cry too.

"I'm really sorry," I sputtered, "but you're going to
have to go to the dance without me." Then I blew
my nose rather loudly. *HONK!*

Chloe and Zoey looked at each other and then looked at me.

"Sorry, Nikki. But we're not going to leave you here like this!" Zoey said, squeezing my hand.

"We care about you! So either we're ALL going to the dance, or we're ALL staying here," Chloe said softly.

"I'll be fine," I protested. "You both have dates. Theo and Marcus are nice guys, and they don't deserve to be stood up. It feels really . . . BAD!"

"Nikki, if you don't want to go, we understand. We'll just call the guys right now and tell them the situation," Zoey said, picking up her phone.

"Please! You're both just making me feel worse!" I yelled. "I want to be ALONE! Just GO AWAY!"

That's when Chloe and Zoey stared at me in disbelief. I think I must have really ticked them off or something because they were not smiling.

"Sorry, Nikki! But we're NOT going to let you have a nervous breakdown over some dude not taking you to a stupid dance!" Chloe fumed.

"So cry yourself a river, build a bridge and get OVER it!" Zoey said, rolling her eyes.

I could NOT believe my BFFs weren't being more sympathetic about my situation. Hey, I was heartbroken and in real pain! Hadn't I earned the right to be a melancholy drama queen?

Note to self: Get a new CRUSH. And some new BFFs!

Even though I was mad at Chloe and Zoey for not joining my pity party, I had to admit they truly cared about me. They were willing to miss the Sweetheart Dance! AND their first dates! I mean, WHO does THAT?!

I sniffed and blew my nose again. *HONK!!*

"Okay, guys! You win! I'll go to the dance. Against my

will. But I'm NOT going to have fun! And you CAN'T make me!" I grumped.

Chloe and Zoey screamed happily and squished me in a hug sandwich.

"You are NOT going to regret this!" Zoey giggled.

"We're going to have a BLAST together!" Chloe squealed.

"I. Can't. BREATHE!" I croaked, gasping for air.

After prying myself out of their hug, I went to the bathroom to wash my face and freshen up for the dance.

OMG! I looked HORRIBLE!

My hair was a mess and my face was streaked with black tears from my mascara.

I looked like a zombie bride or something. . .

SNIFF!
SNIFF!

However, thanks to Chloe and Zoey, I was starting to feel like maybe it WASN'T the end of the world. Most important, I was NOT going to let Brandon turn me into a snivelling puddle of SNOT and TEARS!! Well, not for more than fifteen minutes, anyway.

When we arrived at the Sweetheart Dance, I was surprised to see pretty much the entire student body there.

I barely recognized our drab cafeteria. It had been turned into a Queen of Hearts fantasyland. Dozens of red hearts hung gracefully from the ceiling while bunches of pink, red, and white helium balloons floated gently around the room like miniature clouds. The walls were strung with hundreds of tiny red and white lights that reflected off a giant mirror ball in the centre of the room.

All of the girls wore gorgeous formal dresses that rivaled the dresses at any high school prom. I saw sparkles, glitter, sequins and pretty much every colour of the rainbow.

However, my most favourite dress was my OWN ☺!

Marcus and Theo were there, patiently waiting for Chloe and Zoey. I couldn't tell who was more nervous, my BFFs or their dates. But as soon as they spotted each other, everyone was all smiles.

OMG! They were SO adorable! It was totally worth coming to the dance just to see them together.

"We saved six seats. Right near the wing-dings table!" Theo said, leading the way.

"OMG! I LOVE wing-dings!" I said excitedly.

Dealing with all of that drama and emotional turmoil had pretty much sapped my energy and left me famished. I was STARVING!

It looked like I had a date for the dance after all. I was going to spend most of the evening with a huge plate of yummy wing-dings. Woo-hoo ☺!

Chloe and Zoey glanced at Theo and then whispered to each other.

"Um, Theo? Actually, we'll only need five seats. Brandon's sick. So Nikki will be hanging out with us tonight," Chloe explained.

Theo and Marcus looked at each other and then at us.

"Brandon's sick? Are you sure?" Theo asked.

"YES!" Chloe and Zoey answered tersely.

"But I just saw him five minutes ago. Did he leave or something?" Marcus asked.

"WHAT?!!" Zoey shrieked.

"NO WAY!!" Chloe screeched.

"OMG! Brandon is actually HERE?!" I gasped. "Are you SURE?!"

Theo and Marcus looked at me like I was crazy.

"Yes, we're sure," they replied.

"I can't believe it! WHAT is HE doing here?!" I sputtered.

Theo shrugged. "I think talking to MacKen—"

"MacKenzie?! But he's NOT supposed to be here!" I spat.

294

"He isn't?" Marcus asked.

"NO!" Chloe and Zoey shouted.

"I can't just sit here and pretend like nothing happened!" I fumed.

Basically Brandon had stood me up so MacKenzie could pay HIM to take HER to the dance.

Right then he was the last person I wanted to see.

"But the table is close to the w-wing-dings! Just like Zoey asked!" Theo stammered.

"I think I want to go home," I said, panicking.

Theo looked worried. "Please don't leave, Nikki. I can find us a new table! Maybe near the punch instead of the wing-dings?"

"Actually, Theo, this has absolutely NOTHING to do with wing-dings," Chloe snapped.

"It doesn't?" Theo blinked.

"Brandon told Nikki he was SICK!" Zoey huffed.

"Well, um . . . maybe he IS sick. We didn't really ask him how he was feeling," Marcus muttered.

Suddenly a wave of anger swept over me. "I can't believe Brandon actually lied to me. I need to see this with my own eyes!"

"Okay. Then Zoey and I will come with—" But before Chloe could finish her sentence, I turned and marched across the dance floor.

It was crowded and very dimly lit.

But finally my eyes adjusted to the darkness. Everyone was up dancing to the latest tunes by One Direction and the Wanted. Suddenly I saw the answer to my question just in front of me. Theo and Marcus were right! Brandon WAS, in fact, there . . .

. . . WITH MACKENZIE ☹!!

Blinking back my tears, I quickly turned and walked away before Brandon spotted me.

I brushed past Marcus, Theo, Chloe and Zoey, and then ran out the door and down the hall.

"Nikki! WAIT!" my BFFs called after me.

But I just ignored them.

I rushed straight to the bathroom furthest from the dance and locked myself in the last stall. No one would find me in there. I just wanted to be alone.

Brandon had LIED to me!

He wasn't sick at all. I guess I wasn't pretty or popular enough for him.

Why didn't he just tell me he wanted to go to the dance with MacKenzie? I leaned against the cold stall door as my thoughts raced.

I could feel hot tears trickling down my cheeks.

Just great ☹! The last thing I needed right then was my face covered with black tear stains.

I angrily tugged at the roll of toilet paper and just stared blankly as the paper rolled off.

I was buried knee-deep in paper, but I didn't care.

I grabbed one end and dabbed my eyes and cheeks.

Then I blew my nose.

HONK!!

Suddenly the bathroom door creaked open.

"Do you think she came all the way over here?" Chloe asked.

"It's possible. All of the bathrooms near the dance are pretty crowded," Zoey answered.

"Hey, I think you're right," Chloe said. "Look under that stall. Only Nikki would use that much toilet paper!"

They whispered to each other, then knocked on my stall door. I opened it a few inches and peeked out.

"GO AWAY!" I said glumly.

"Nikki, we are SO sorry about all of this! We had no idea Brandon was here," Chloe said.

"Hey! It's not your fault that Brandon is a lying rat!" I fumed.

"You need to forget him! The sooner the better!" Zoey said.

Of course I choked up again when I heard that.

"We're only telling you this because we care about you," Chloe said. "Just breathe, okay? Can I get you anything? A bottled water? Are you hungry?"

How could I possibly think about food when my whole world was crashing in on my head? "Actually, I want to go home now. I'm going to call my mom."

"We totally understand," Zoey said sadly. "This whole evening has been a nightmare!"

"Well, the least we can do is go grab you some wing-dings to take home with you. We'll be right back," Chloe said.

Actually, a huge plate of wing-dings sounded pretty good.

"Thanks, guys. I could eat a horse," I muttered.

I was alone in the bathroom again with nothing but my jumbled thoughts.

What had turned Brandon into such a JERK that he would text-dump me less than an hour before the Sweetheart Dance?

MacKenzie!

Her plan had totally worked. Brandon had ripped out my heart, threw it in the dirt and trampled all over it. Just like she wanted! And now they were probably flirting with each other during a slow dance!

UGHHH!!!!

I picked up my phone to call my mom but was interrupted by a loud commotion. Chloe and Zoey came storming back into the bathroom.

"Nikki!" Zoey shrieked. "You are NOT going to believe this! Brandon just walked up to us and asked us where you were. He says he's been waiting for you!"

"What?!" I poked my head out of my stall. "Are you kidding me?!"

"OMG! I was livid!" Chloe fumed. "So I said to him, 'You can keep waiting until heck freezes over! You're just a phoney, backstabbing slimeball who is supposed to be at home SICK!'"

"And get this! He said he didn't have the slightest idea what we were talking about!" Zoey said.

"How could he just LIE right to our faces like that?" Chloe ranted. "That's when I said really

sweetly, 'Okay, Brandon, maybe a refreshing drink
will help clear up your foggy memory!'"

"OMG! You actually said that to him?" I gasped.
"Then what happened?"

"I had to grab the Karate Kid before she dumped a
cup of punch over his head and gave him a
beatdown," Zoey said, glaring at Chloe.

← CHLOE, THE
KARATE KID

"Hey! Give me a break!" Chloe shot back. "I was trying to get a drink and he just happened to be in my way! Anything I almost did to him was purely accidental."

"Chloe, just calm down! You're not making this any better," I scolded.

"You know what would make ME feel better? How about I 'accidentally' sock Brandon in the stomach?"

"Chloe, you can't just walk up to a person and sock him in his stomach," Zoey said. "There are laws against that!"

"Okay, then. How about I punch him in the nose?! Or give him a kick in the butt? He totally deserves that and more!"

"Chloe! This is a middle school dance, not the HUNGER GAMES!" I yelled. "I want to go HOME. Not to JAIL!"

Finally she regained her composure. "Sorry, Nikki!

I just temporarily lost it," she said quietly.

But I'd already had enough.

"Listen, guys! This is NUTS! I need to get out of here. I'm going to call my mom and have her pick me up. But the last person I want to see or talk to is Brandon."

"Yeah, and he definitely doesn't want to see ME!" Chloe said, making a fist and cracking her knuckles.

"Okay, Nikki. Chloe and I will go out and make sure the coast is clear. Then you can make your getaway. We'll be right back."

I glanced at myself in the mirror. I was a mess. But I put on two layers of lip gloss and gathered up all of my stuff, including my courage.

I was SO ready to leave that smelly stall.

Chloe and Zoey almost broke down the door rushing back into the bathroom.

"Nikki, you're not going to believe what just happened!" Chloe screeched.

I rolled my eyes. "Please don't tell me you punched Brandon."

"Actually, I DIDN'T. But I REALLY, REALLY wanted to!" Chloe growled.

"We just saw Brandon again!" Zoey panted. "He says he wants to talk to you!"

I started to panic. "NO! I can't talk to him right now! You guys didn't tell him where I was, did you?!"

"Of course not!" they answered.

"I've tried really hard to be friends with Brandon. And after Crazy Burger, I thought we'd finally worked things out. But I give up! He has made me cry, upset my best friends, ruined the Sweetheart Dance, killed what little self-respect I had and, and, um . . . driven me temporarily INSANE!"

"Nikki, don't say that about yourself," Zoey said quietly. "You're NOT insane!"

"JUST LOOK AT ME! Not only do I look like a zombie bride, but I'm having a complete meltdown. In a bathroom stall! While buried in a roll of toilet paper!"

"OMG!" Chloe quipped. "You ARE insane!"

"We're really sorry, Nikki! We shouldn't have made you come to the dance against your will," Zoey mumbled.

"Don't be sorry," I replied. "It's good that I finally learned the truth about Brandon. I just wish he had the decency to tell me himself, face-to-face."

"I WOULD if you'd let me!" said a voice outside the bathroom door.

"BRANDON?!" I sputtered. "OMG!"

"I didn't tell him you were hiding out in here! I swear!" Zoey whispered to me.

"Don't look at me!" Chloe whisper-shouted. "I don't talk to pathological liars!"

"Actually, I just followed Chloe and Zoey over here," Brandon said. "Nikki, will you please come out so we can talk?!"

"There's nothing to talk about," I shot back. "Just leave me alone. You should have just told me you wanted to go to the dance with MacKenzie and saved me a lot of heartache."

"Nikki, YOU asked me to this dance. I think you owe me an explanation for why you decided to stand me up!" Brandon said.

"What?! I didn't stand YOU up! You stood ME up! But I don't want to talk about any of this. You're supposed to be home sick with the flu! Remember?" I yelled through the bathroom door.

"Okay, fine! If you're not coming OUT, then I'm coming IN," Brandon said.

Chloe, Zoey, and I were speechless.

"NO WAY! He CAN'T be serious!" I finally gasped.

We stared at the door in disbelief as it slowly creaked open and Brandon peeked in.

His face was flushed, and he looked totally bewildered.

I could NOT believe he'd actually come inside the girls' bathroom to talk to me.

"I can't believe I'm actually inside the girls' bathroom. But I really need to talk to you!" he muttered.

Chloe and Zoey were about to protest.

But I think Brandon looked so utterly embarrassed that they felt kind of sorry for him.

"If anyone catches me in here, I'll probably get detention for a month!" he said, looking around nervously. "Anyway, I really apologise for coming in here, but I'm desperate!"

"Actually, Chloe and I were just leaving," Zoey said.

"I'M not going anywhere," Chloe said, folding her arms. "There's no way I'd miss any of THIS! I wish

311

I had a bucket of popcorn and some gummy bears."

"Chloe! Let's go!" Zoey said sternly.

She grabbed Chloe's arm and dragged her through the door.

"OW! That hurt!" Chloe complained, rubbing her arm.

Chloe turned around and shot Brandon a dirty look. "Hey, dude, you better watch your step. We'll be standing right outside this door. Listening!"

"Um, Chloe, don't worry. I'll be just fine. Really!" I assured her.

Once Brandon and I were alone, my heart started pounding and my palms got sweaty.

"Nikki . . . you've been acting kind of strange ever since my birthday," Brandon said. "But I don't understand why."

"ME?! YOU'VE been acting strange lately," I

said, trying to swallow the lump in my throat. "And those text messages! They've been just . . . CRUEL!"

"Text messages? What text messages?!"

"Don't pretend you didn't send them!" I glared at him. "They came directly from your phone. At first I didn't want to believe you gave MacKenzie that crazy picture of me, but now I'm starting to wonder. If you don't want to be friends with me anymore, just say so!"

"Nikki, it seems like YOU don't want to be friends with ME. One minute you're fine and the next minute you're mad at me. This whole month has been crazy! I thought maybe it had to do with the Sweetheart Dance or something."

My phone chimed and I pulled it out of my bag.

It was yet another text message from Brandon.

"See? This is EXACTLY what I'm talking about. I'm

really tired of your texts. Seriously!" I said, pointing to my phone.

ME, PUTTING BRANDON ON BLAST
BECAUSE I'M SICK AND TIRED OF
HIS SORTA WEIRD AND SLIGHTLY
OFFENSIVE TEXT MESSAGES

"Um, Nikki! You have a problem. I've been HERE in the GIRLS' BATHROOM talking to YOU for the past three minutes."

"*I* have a problem?! Really? You're the dude sneaking into the GIRLS' bathroom! Obviously, YOU have a problem!! Have you considered counselling?"

"Nikki! How could *I* have just sent YOU a TEXT?! Did you see me do it?" he asked.

"Huh?" I muttered, staring at my phone.

Okay, now I was totally confused.

"Then WHO just sent me this text?!"

I opened the message on my phone and read it out loud: "I'm so sorry about the dance. But I just coughed up what looked like a big slimy greenish booger and thought of you!"

Then I handed my phone to Brandon so he could read the text that had come from HIS phone.

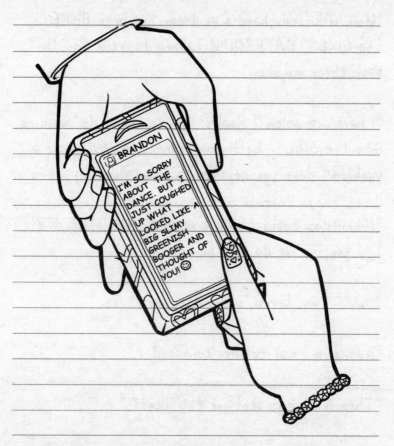

I'M SO SORRY ABOUT THE DANCE. BUT I JUST COUGHED UP WHAT LOOKED LIKE A BIG SLIMY GREENISH BOOGER AND THOUGHT OF YOU! 🙂

BRANDON

He read the message scowled and shook his head.

"So that text is supposed to be from ME?" Brandon asked. "Come on! Do you think I would actually talk about something as crass and juvenile as boogers? And when have I EVER used a smiley face? I'm really sorry you had to go through all of this, Nikki."

"Well, if these texts aren't from you, then WHO is sending them? And WHY are they coming from YOUR phone?"

"I don't know. But what I do know is that I COULDN'T have sent them because I lost my phone a month ago! It's been missing since my party. Since Theo's brother has a phone just like mine, we thought maybe he'd accidentally taken it back to college or something."

A wave of relief washed over me.

So Brandon had NOT been sending all of those crazy text messages for the past month! Maybe we could actually salvage our friendship after all.

"Well, that makes me feel a lot better. But why didn't you just tell me you lost your phone?"

"Because you never gave me a chance. I missed going to Crazy Burger with you the first time because Theo and I were searching all over the place for my phone. I tried to apologise and explain everything that next day at school, but you blew me off," he said.

"Okay, so maybe part of the misunderstanding was MY fault. I'm sorry. But why were you hanging out with MacKenzie just now?"

"You're right. I was talking to MacKenzie earlier tonight. But she came up to me, not the other way around. She told me you were home sick with the flu and wouldn't be coming to the dance."

"Wait a minute! I got a text message right before the dance saying the exact same thing! That YOU had the flu and couldn't make it!"

"You're kidding! So you thought I was just NOT going to show up?" Brandon asked.

"To be honest, I didn't know what to think! I wanted to stay home, but Chloe and Zoey dragged me here. And when I saw you here with MacKenzie when you were supposed to be home sick, I got a little upset!"

"A little?!"

"Okay! I TOTALLY lost it!!" I admitted.

"Well, I knew you'd never just stand me up like that! That's why I asked Chloe and Zoey if you were here. Zoey gave me the stink eye and Chloe went nuts and tried to dump a cup of punch over my head. It was scary!"

"I'm really sorry. That was probably my fault. I guess they were mad at you because of all the things I'd said about you."

"Well, I'd feel a lot safer if you told your BFFs to back off. Anyway, I'm really glad we talked. Now maybe things can get back to normal."

"Yeah, but we still don't know who is behind those text messages or how they got your phone," I said. "Although, I think I have a hunch who's probably responsible."

"Me too. My phone seemed to disappear around the

319

same time MacKenzie left my party that night.
But we need proof she has it."

We just stared at my phone and racked our brains.
And the more times we read that nasty text message,
the more angry and frustrated we became . . .

That's when the most brilliant idea popped into my head.

It was the perfect prank and would expose the culprit.

And all I had to do was send a very simple text message. To . . . BRANDON!

* * * * *
FROM NIKKI:
Hi Brandon,
I know you were happy about MacKenzie's generous offer to help Fuzzy Friends. But I think buying her that diamond necklace from Tiffany & Co. as a thank you gift was a bit much. Anyway, I went ahead and gift-wrapped it like you asked me. But I placed it in #1573 (behind the school), which is exactly where it belongs.
Sorry ☹!
8:17 p.m.
* * * * *

Now all we had to do was wait patiently for the perpetrator to take the bait.

Brandon smiled at me. "Nikki, you're an evil genius. So, now that we've squashed all the drama, are you and I . . . cool again?"

"Sure! We're cool!" I said, blushing.

"Great. Let's get the heck out of here. Friends don't let friends hide out in the girls' bathroom!"

Then we both laughed really hard at Brandon's joke.

Chloe, Zoey, Brandon and I walked back to the dance together and joined Theo and Marcus at our table.

When I told my BFFs about the mysterious text messages and Brandon's lost phone, they could hardly believe it.

Anyway, we pigged out on wing-dings. And the fancy catered dinner was fabulous too.

I couldn't believe an evening that had started out

so horribly wrong had turned out to be so . . . wonderful!

But mostly I was SUPERhappy that we were all finally getting along again, just like old times.

Okay! I had learned my lesson. I would NEVER, EVER doubt Brandon's friendship again, I told myself.

"Oh, Brandon! There you are!" MacKenzie squealed. "I've been looking all over for you!"

She was really surprised to see me sitting there. "OMG! Nikki!" She sneered. "What are YOU doing here? I thought you were home sick. You're obviously coming down with something! Your face looks like death on a STICK! I hope it's not contagious."

I just rolled my eyes at that girl.

"BTW, I have a little surprise for you. Apparently, a few of your so-called friends have been handing out copies of that hideous picture of you behind your back. I just wanted to let you know. Hey, with friends like those, who needs enemies? Anyway, I thought I'd give you this one to hang in your locker!" Then she shoved a poster right in my face. . .

"We ripped down the posters YOU put up! No real friend of mine would do that to me!" I shot back.

"Oh, really?" MacKenzie said, and stared right at Brandon! "I guess you never know who you can trust! Right, Brandon?"

"MacKenzie, you're such a liar! Brandon would never do something like that!" I argued.

Brandon looked really uncomfortable and glared at MacKenzie. But I noticed that for some reason, he avoided looking at me. Why was he acting so . . . guilty?

MacKenzie laughed. "He was giving them out to people right under your nose!"

"Brandon, WHAT is she talking about?" I was starting to get upset all over again.

"I had absolutely nothing to do with the posters that were plastered up last week. But MacKenzie's right. I have to admit, this one is mine . . ." Brandon said, hanging his head.

I stared at him in shock! Just when I had decided to trust him again, he was acting like a total JERK!

"How could you do this to me?" I cried. "The last thing I need is dozens more of those pictures floating around the school!"

"Dozens?! Marcus and I helped Brandon hand out at least three hundred of them. That picture is too hilarious!" Theo laughed. "Everybody wanted one."

"Marcus, how could you?!" Chloe exclaimed in shock.

"Theo, that's just CRUEL!" Zoey said, shaking her head in disgust.

I stood up abruptly to leave. "Sorry! I've had enough! I'm out of here!"

"Wait, Nikki. We're coming with you," Chloe said.

"Let's go get our coats," Zoey huffed.

"Wait, just let me explain!" Brandon pleaded.

"There's NO excuse for what you did!" I scolded, blinking back tears for what seemed like the fifth time tonight. "It wasn't funny!"

Suddenly the house lights came on and Principal Winston took the stage.

"Okay, students! May I have your attention, please? It's time to crown our WCD Sweetheart Princess."

"OMG!" MacKenzie shrieked. "They're about to announce the Sweetheart Princess. I'm pretty sure I won. Anyway, I gotta go. They're going to need me onstage. LATER, HATERS!" Then she sashayed away. I just HATE it when that girl sashays!

Mr Winston continued. "First I'd like to thank our maths teacher, Mrs Sprague, for counting all of the ballots earlier today. Now I am very proud and honoured to announce that our new WCD Sweetheart Princess is . . ."

MacKenzie Hollister, I grumbled inside my head. It's ALWAYS MacKenzie Hollister!

"NIKKI MAXWELL!! CONGRATULATIONS!!"

OMG! I could not believe my ears! I just stood there in total shock with my mouth hanging open.

If Chloe and Zoey hadn't been holding on to me, I would have fallen right over.

How could this have happened? And why would anyone vote for me, the BIGGEST DORK in the entire school?

That's when Brandon brushed his shaggy hair out of his eyes and gave me a crooked smile. Then he turned the poster over and handed it to me . . .

OMG! My eyes almost popped out of my head! It said nice stuff about ME. Only no one had bothered to tell ME about it. Or my BFFs, Chloe and Zoey. Finally it all made sense why kids had been whispering about me at school today.

"Would Nikki and her date please come up to the stage?" Mr Winston asked. "We have a special gift for you, young lady!"

As the entire student body cheered (well, everyone except MacKenzie, who was staring at her phone), Brandon and I made our way to the stage.

It felt like I was in a dream. I carefully opened a white box and inside was the most beautiful tiara I'd ever seen!

OMG! Brandon was the perfect escort.

He even helped me with my tiara.

Okay, he placed it on my head totally lopsided!

But STILL! It's the thought that counts.

After that, each couple at the dance got to pose for a really nice keepsake picture. It felt like we were at a senior prom or something. . .

CHLOE AND MARCUS ☺!

ZOEY AND THEO ☺!

And last but not least . . .

ME AND BRANDON ☺!!

I thought all of our photos came out SUPERcute!

Then, thanks to Jordyn, we FINALLY learned the identity of the mysterious person who had stolen Brandon's phone and sent me those messages . . .

OMG! LOOK OUTSIDE!

Not that we were all that shocked and surprised . . .

"WHERE'S MY PRESENT FROM BRANDON?!!
IT'S JUST GOT TO BE IN HERE SOMEWHERE!!"

Soon the lights went down and the disco ball lit up for a slow dance.

Brandon kept staring at me with this strange look on his face. Then he nervously cleared his throat.

"Wow, Nikki! I've been wanting to tell you that you look . . . um, totally . . . !!" Brandon's mouth opened but no words came out. I guess he was speechless.

"Thank you," I gushed. "And I wanted to say that you look beyond awesome!"

"Thank you!" Brandon said shyly. "So . . . uh . . . do you wanna . . . ?" He nodded toward the dance floor.

"Sure. I'd love to," I answered, and took his hand.

We danced, laughed and spoke to each other in what probably sounded like gibberish for the rest of the evening. But we understood each other perfectly.

It was the most sweetly AWKWARD and insanely BEAUTIFUL moment of my entire LIFE!

It was like I was a princess in my very OWN fairy tale.

And Brandon was my handsome prince and a very cool friend. I was finally having my dorkily ever after and I wanted this moment to last forever.

Suddenly I remembered that most of my favourite fairy tales ended with the prince and princess sharing a romantic KISS!!

So of course I TOTALLY FREAKED during our very last dance! And guess what happened?!! OMG! I was so nervous I thought I was going to pee my pants. Which, BTW, wasn't the first time, and definitely NOT the last!

I can't wait to share ALL of the exciting details! SQUEEE!!

TOMORROW!!

Sorry! I'm SUCH a DORK!
☺!!

Hey, you!

Wanna take a sneak peek at a few pages of my next diary, *TV Star*?

Shhhh! It's a secret . . .

SATURDAY, MARCH 1

OMG!! I STILL can hardly believe what happened to me yesterday!! THREE totally-awesome-completely-unbelievable-too-good-to-be-true-exciting-wonderful things!!

Totally-awesome-completely-unbelievable-too-good-to-be-true-exciting-wonderful thing #1: I ACTUALLY WENT TO THE VALENTINE'S DAY SWEETHEART DANCE ☺!! SQUEEEE!

Yep! It was girls ask the guys! And at the very last moment, I FINALLY got up the nerve to ask my crush, Brandon!

Totally-awesome-completely-unbelievable-too-good-to-be-true-exciting-wonderful thing #2: I WAS CROWNED SWEETHEART PRINCESS ☺!! SQUEEEEEEEE!!

I still don't know exactly how THAT happened. But it did! And I have my TIARA to prove it!!

And finally, the most AMAZING thing EVER!

SQUEEEEEEEEEEEEE!!!

Totally-awesome-completely-unbelievable-too-good-to-be-true-exciting-wonderful thing #3: DURING THE VERY LAST DANCE OF THE MOST PERFECT, ROMANTIC, FAIRY-TALE EVENING, BRANDON AND I . . .

Hey! Wait a minute! Is that my cell phone ringing?!!

YES! My phone IS ringing!!!

Hey! Maybe it's . . .

BRANDON!! ☺!!!

(Checking my caller ID . . .)

NOPE!! It's NOT Brandon calling.

WAIT!! OMG!!! I can't believe it's . . .

He's just THE most famous TV producer in the entire WORLD! And the host of my FAVORITE TV show, a reality TV show/talent boot camp called . . .

15 Minutes of FAME

SQUEEEEEEE ☺!!

Gotta answer my phone!

I'm on spring break from school this entire week. So I'll have plenty of time to finish writing this . . .

LATER!!! ☺!

OMG! Saturday night was a complete NIGHTMARE!! How bad was it? SO bad I'm breaking into a cold sweat and having traumatic flashbacks just writing about it.

AAAAAAAAAAAAHHH! That was me screaming!! Sorry!! Must. Stop. Screaming! Anyway . . .

I can hardly believe the KA-RAY-ZEE mess I got myself into THIS time!

I wondered if they allowed diaries in JAIL! Because that's exactly where I was headed. No JOKE!! The authorities were about to place me under arrest ☹! But girlfriend wasn't going down without a fight!

And by fight, I mean trying to figure out whether I could sneak out of a nearby window, crawl onto a six-inch ledge, dangle by my fingertips over a railing, and then jump five floors to the ground below . . . without SPLATTERING myself all over the parking lot!!

Hmm . . . ?!

Probably . . . NOT ☹!!

But it gets worse! My BFFs, Chloe and Zoey, were getting arrested too. And it was all MY fault!

I was such a HORRIBLE person! I TOTALLY deserved it if they UNFRIENDED me on Facebook!

If only I HADN'T dragged them into this MESS!

I was just minding my own business and writing in my diary when I got that call Saturday morning. . . .

"Hello, Nikki! Great news! I'm in town today with my new group, the BAD BOYZ! I'd love to meet with you to discuss recording your band's song 'Dorks Rule!' The only problem is that we'll be leaving soon to go on a world tour. So I can only meet with you TONIGHT. Otherwise, it'll be about seven months before my schedule clears up again. Do you think you can make it to the Bad Boyz concert tonight?"

"OMG! Mr. Chase?! Yes, I'd love to! But that concert sold out months ago in, like, ten minutes. My two BFFs camped out in line overnight and STILL couldn't get any tickets."

"No problem! I'll give you three backstage passes so you can bring a couple of your band members. Just pick them up at the reserved-tickets window, okay?"

That was when I completely FAINTED! Well, actually, ALMOST completely fainted.

"Backstage passes?! That's AWESOME! Thank you, Mr. Chase! I'll see you TONIGHT!"

I could NOT believe this was happening! My band, Actually, I'm Not Really Sure Yet, might get a record deal! I hung up the phone and immediately called Chloe and Zoey to see if they wanted to go to the concert.

They answered with one word: "SQUEEEEE!" ☺!!

We all agreed it was going to be the MOST fun we'd had together since, um . . . yesterday!

When we arrived at the arena, we waited in line with THOUSANDS of excited fans. But you'd NEVER guess who we just happened to run into on our way to the ticket window. . . .

MACKENZIE ☹!!!

Don't miss more diaries

Dork Diaries

Dork Diaries: Party Time

Dork Diaries: Pop Star

Dork Diaries: Skating Sensation

Dork Diaries: Dear Dork

Dork Diaries: Holiday Heartbreak

by Rachel Renée Russell!

MOST IMPORTANT TIP EVER FROM NIKKI MAXWELL:

Always let your inner **DORK** shine through!

#1 New York Times Bestselling Series

Dork Diaries: TV Star

Dork Diaries: Once Upon a Dork

Dork Diaries: Drama Queen

Dork Diaries: Puppy Love

Dork Diaries: OMG! All About Me Diary

Dork Diaries: How to Dork Your Diary

Do you love

DORK diaries

and reading all about Nikki's not-so-fabulous life??

Then don't miss out on the BRAND NEW series from **Rachel Renée Russell!** featuring new dork on the block,

MAX CRUMBLY!

Rachel Renée Russell

the misadventures of MAX CRUMBLY

Locker Hero

from the creator of DORK diaries

"If you like Tom Gates,
Diary of A Wimpy Kid and, of course,
Dork Diaries you'll love this!" *The Sun*

Rachel Renée Russell is the #1 *New York Times* bestselling author of the block-buster book series Dork Diaries and the exciting new series The Misadventures of Max Crumbly.

There are more than twenty-five million copies of her books in print worldwide, and they have been translated into thirty-six languages.

She enjoys working with her two daughters, Erin and Nikki, who help write and illustrate her books.

Rachel's message is "Become the hero you've always admired!"